HUNTER

A DS Hunter Kerr Prequel

Michael Fowler

SAPERE
BOOKS

HUNTER

Published by Sapere Books.

20 Windermere Drive, Leeds, England, LS17 7UZ,
United Kingdom

saperebooks.com

ISBN: 978-1-913335-25-0

This is dedicated to the memory of my parents, John and Dulcie, whose gift of a typewriter on my 15th Christmas, set me on the road to achieve my dreams of becoming a writer.

CHAPTER ONE

Barnwell, Yorkshire, 1991

Taking refuge in the doorway of the Yorkshire Bank on Barnwell High Street, Police Constable Hunter Kerr gazed out over the sodden street. The rain had halted but the night sky still rumbled and threatened as the storm of twenty minutes ago petered away into the next valley. The deluge had left behind oily black pools upon which irregular rainbow patterns played along the surface. In the distance the church bell struck midnight.

Hunter's stomach felt uncomfortable, though not from nervousness — it was the meal he had just eaten, stodgy cottage pie, which was now repeating itself. It had felt strange eating a microwave meal that late at night — especially when sober. He vowed that his food choice for the remainder of the week would consist only of light snacks.

A hand tapped him on the shoulder, bringing his senses back to the moment.

'Come back into the shadows, you'll never catch anyone standing out like that.' Roger Mills' voice was a gruff whisper.

Hunter stepped back and brushed shoulders with his tutor constable. He said softly, 'It's quiet.'

Roger nudged him with his elbow. 'Wash your mouth out with soapy water, young Kerr. You're risking fate saying that. Believe me, once you've had a few years of Friday and Saturday nights under your belt, you'll savour moments like this.'

Hunter took in his mentor's features. Craggy-faced with dark cropped hair, Roger Mills was an ex-paratrooper, who had served in Northern Ireland before becoming a cop 14 years ago, and he still paraded himself with all the bearings of a military man. It was Hunter's fifth week with his tutor, and second tour of nights, and he'd already learned from others in his group that he couldn't have wished to have been teamed up with anyone better.

'It's usually at this time when I start asking all my student officers why on earth they joined this god-forsaken job,' Roger said, 'but I heard you telling Andy Sharp the other day that you had planned to go to university but changed your mind. What on earth made you do that? If you'd have joined the force with a degree, you would have gone into the fast-track system, been a sergeant in five years and an inspector in 10. A lot cushier than walking the streets like I'm going to have to do for the next 30 years.'

That unexpected question instantly pricked Hunter's conscience. Devastated by the brutal murder of his first love, Polly, and vowing to catch her killer, he had joined the rough, tough environment of policing, aged 19. He had been one of the youngest recruits on his police training school intake and took a lot of ribbing for his clean-shaven, fresh-faced appearance, and gangly 10-stone frame. His class instructors did their level best to embarrass him over his naive approach to some of the training exercises but he managed to put up a spirited resistance, as well as withstanding the continuous bawling and berating from the 'drill-pig' during early morning parades, when he struggled with marching.

By the end of the 10 weeks, Hunter had proved he could survive both mentally and physically, and his performance shortlisted him for Course Best Student, in which disappointingly for him, he came runner-up.

Following training, Hunter was surprised, but pleased, to learn that he had been posted to his home town of Barnwell, in the Dearne Valley of South Yorkshire; a district steeped in working-class culture, and one slowly recovering from the demise of centuries of heavy industry, especially coal mining. And, although he knew that it was going to be hard, because of the community's dislike of police officers following the Miner's Strike, he was determined to prove himself worthy of wearing his uniform and put a foothold on the possibility of a 30-year career.

Hunter pulled back his gaze and stared at the glistening wet pavement. 'My girlfriend was murdered,' he told Roger softly. He felt a lump emerge into his throat and swallowed hard. It had been three years since Polly's death, but he still felt sick to his stomach whenever he thought about it. 'I promised her parents I'd catch the person who did it.'

Roger was quiet for a moment. Then he said, 'I didn't expect that for an answer. When did this happen?'

Hunter bit down on his lip. 'First of September, 1988.' The date was carved into his memory.

'And it was never solved?'

'Nope.'

'Did it happen round here?'

Hunter nodded. 'Close to the woods near Roman Ridge.'

'Not Polly Hayes!'

Hunter met Roger's eyes. 'You knew her?'

Roger shook his head. 'Not personally I didn't, but I was on duty that day when the call came in from her parents saying their dog had come home alone with blood covering its fur and collar. As you know, we usually don't do anything for 24 hours, especially given Polly's age, but the blood on the dog scaled everything up a notch. I was one of the officers who went out searching for her. We found her body up near the woods. That was her, wasn't it?'

Hunter nodded in the darkness. Suddenly, ghost-like, a vision of Polly drifted inside his head. She was giving him one of her mischievous smiles. It was a fleeting glimpse and then she was gone again. The flashes of Polly coming back to visit him were becoming less frequent. Hunter wondered if there ever would be a time when he could no longer imagine her. He stared out across the glistening tarmac. A gush of wind ripped down the street, creating small waves across the puddles.

'It was a real shocker finding her like that, I can tell you.' Tight-mouthed, Roger shook his head, 'Fancy Polly being your girlfriend. Small world.' Pausing, he added, 'You must have been devastated.'

Roger's words brought Hunter back from his reverie. 'I was. It's not something you ever imagine happening to you.'

'You still think about it?'

'Most of the time.'

Roger held Hunter's gaze for a few seconds, then said, 'I didn't stay on that job. Our shift got involved in the initial search, and I spoke to a couple of people who'd been in the vicinity at the time, but that was all. CID took over. I remember that the Incident Room was busy for a good six months, but I can't recall there ever being a main suspect, and if my memory serves me right the investigation was wound down after 12 months. Which, I'm guessing, given that she was your girlfriend, must have left you gutted?'

'It did. It was especially bad for her parents. Me and my mates were among the people who got grilled over her murder.'

'You mean as suspects?'

'Yep. I was interviewed three times.'

Roger let out a quick laugh.

'It's not funny. It was scary. I was only 16. I felt as though everyone was thinking it was me and there were days I wouldn't even go out of the house. It wasn't a nice feeling at all.'

Roger's face straightened. 'No, I suppose not.' After a short pause, he said, 'I'm surprised, given what you went through, that you wanted to join this job. You can't have had a good impression of the police if you were treated as a suspect. Who interviewed you?'

'A Detective Newstead. Barry Newstead.'

Roger gave off another sharp snort. 'My God! You must have really gone through the mill, knowing what I know about Barry. I can imagine he gave you a bit of a hard time.'

'An understatement. At one stage, he threatened to lock me up and throw away the key. He scared the shit out of me.'

Roger let out another short laugh. 'That sounds like Barry.'

Hunter was quiet for a moment. Then he said, 'Have you ever been a suspect over anything, Roger?'

'Not for something as serious as that, I haven't. I was disciplined a few times when I was in the army for fighting. And, in this job, I've been interviewed a couple of times by The Rubber-heeled Squad when prisoners have made complaints. That wasn't much fun, I can tell you.' Pausing momentarily, he added, 'Anyway, you're here now and in the job. Hopefully you'll be able to keep your promise to Polly's parents.'

They fell silent for the best part of a minute, then Roger said softly, 'It may not be any consolation, but I've also lost some good friends over the years, especially when I was in Northern Ireland, and although I never forget them, it does get easier with time. The other thing I will say to you, Hunter, is don't mix up the experience of Polly's death with what you are going to face in the future. Dealing with death is something we do on a regular basis in this job. If I can give you any advice, it's to distance yourself and don't make it personal. Your role is to note down the circumstances and gather the evidence. That's it. If after your first couple of deaths you're struggling to separate your emotions, then this is not the job for you.'

Hunter turned and met Roger's gaze.

Cracking a smile, Roger said, 'Anyway, young Kerr, enough of my pearls of wisdom. Let's get back to keeping an eye on things.'

Hunter's radio suddenly crackled into life. The operator's voice had some urgency, and as her message tailed off, he felt Roger nudge him in his side.

'Come on, someone's fallen in the ponds. We're the nearest.'

Picking up his pace, Hunter followed close to Roger's heels, though, because of his higher fitness level, he found himself overtaking as they neared the location.

Turning the corner of a row of terraces, Hunter entered the dirt track which led to the fishing ponds and he caught his first sight of the black water shimmering under the clouded moon. He put in a burst and heard Roger's panting breath falling back. Within seconds, he had a full view of the fishing lakes layout and urgently scanned the rippling surface. It didn't take him long to spy the darkened shape, arms outstretched, floating away from the banking. The figure was inactive and Hunter's mind began to whirl as an uneasy feeling began to envelop him.

Glancing backwards, he saw Roger at least a hundred yards away.

'Go on, Hunter,' Roger shouted. 'I'll call for back up.'

Hunter's hat was the first item to be discarded, quickly followed by his coat. With his head pounding, he pitched himself into the pond, his feet squelching into thick mud. The shock of the ice-cold water took his breath away, but then adrenaline took over as he began wading towards the motionless floating body.

Roger's torchlight flicked before him, quickly followed by more lights, criss-crossing, from all sides of the banking. Hunter was amazed at the quick response from his group.

As he reached out and grasped the body's sleeve, he shuddered. Not with the cold this time, but at the uncanny stiffness and rigidity of the out-flung arm. Turning over the body, he realised why everyone had appeared so quickly.

The plastic face of a mannequin stared back at him with an almost mocking Mona Lisa smile.

Laughter burst out around him.

Spinning around, a mix of anger and embarrassment engulfing him, the dazzling torch lights blinded him. Hunter could feel the cold seeping into his frame again as he listened to the chuckles of his colleagues dying away. Then he heard the distinctive gruff voice of his tutor.

'I bet you won't be complaining about how quiet things are again.' There was a pause, before Roger added, 'Welcome to the shift, young Kerr.'

CHAPTER TWO

Still secretly smarting from the initiation prank that had left him soaking earlier that week, Hunter patrolled the remainder of his first night week conjuring up ways to retaliate. He was thinking of a way to get his tutor back when his concentration was disturbed by a message on his radio. The operator informed him that they'd received two calls, the first, that a man had been seen on the roof of an outbuilding near the Barnwell Main Hotel — The Drum, as it was known locally — and the second, that an ambulance was attending a collapse near the same location.

In less than five minutes, Hunter and Roger were approaching the old Victorian pub. The two-storey building at the end of the main street was in darkness. Hunter knew The Drum by reputation. He was well aware that many of the clientele who frequented it had fearful past reputations, either as villains, or fighters, or in many cases, both.

Checking the front door and finding it locked, Hunter and Roger skirted around the side of the building to the enclosed rear compound where there were a number of outbuildings. Turning the corner of the pub they were greeted by an uninterrupted cry of pain which appeared to be coming from a dark corner of the yard.

At first glance, all Hunter saw was what looked like a crumpled pile of rags, but as his eyes adjusted, he noticed a slight movement amongst them and he edged closer. As he drew near the bleating grew more intense. He flicked on his torch and his beam picked out a man's grubby face surrounded by a mop of greying ginger hair.

A hand flew up to cover the face.

'I'm crippled. I can't move my bloody legs.'

Hunter stepped forwards and knelt over the prostrate man. 'What's happened?'

'Fell off the fucking roof.' A dirty soiled hand with bloodied fingertips pointed skywards, and Hunter followed the line of the man's arm up the rough brickwork of the outbuilding for some twenty feet where it reached the flat roof.

Returning a surprised look, Hunter said, 'From up there?'

The man nodded and moaned again.

Hunter was suddenly conscious of Roger leaning over his shoulder.

In his gruff drawl, Roger said, 'Now then, Jud, what's appertaining?'

'Fell off the roof, Mr Mills. Bloody hell! I'm really fucking done for this time.'

'What were you doing up there in the first place? Nicking lead, I suppose?'

'Mr Mills, how can you say such a thing!' — a dry barking cough interrupted the flow of words — 'I've been going straight for ages now.'

Hunter's eyes darted between Roger and the inconsolable ginger-haired man. Roger winked at him. Setting his gaze back upon the man, he said, 'Jud, pull the other one. You going straight! You don't know the meaning of the word. You can't even lie in bed straight.'

The man stirred and moaned loudly, 'On my dear mum's life.'

'Jud, your mum's been dead at least five years, to my knowledge.'

'I'll never walk again, Mr Mills, have some sympathy.'

'Luck would be a fine thing. Now let's drop the bullshit and tell us what you were doing up there.'

A coughing fit followed, intermingled with spluttering noises and the odd cry out of pain before the man answered, 'It was like this, sir. You remember my mum.' He paused. 'God rest her soul. Well, the last thing she said to me on her death bed, was look after Bill — that's her budgie, named after my dad. As much as I'm no bird lover, I couldn't let her down, so that's what I've been doing.'

'Where the fuck is this all going, Jud?'

'I'm just getting to that.' Jud winced. 'Tonight he was having his usual fly round the house and I'd forgotten I'd left the window open. He got out, didn't he! Flew straight out, quick as a flash, and when I goes out after him, there he was — up on this roof. He'd be ragged to death by the other birds in the morning if he stayed there, so I climbed up to rescue him and just as I reached to get him, he flew off again. I over-balanced, didn't I, and here I am crippled for the sake of my dear mum's budgie.'

Roger's mouth creased into a smirk. 'I'll give you your due, Jud, you can certainly spin them.'

'It's the God's honest truth, Mr Mills.' With that the man settled back his head and issued a long moan. He only stopped when an ambulance appeared on scene.

Ten minutes later, despite the paramedics carrying a thorough head, neck and spinal check, and finding no major injuries, the man insisted that he needed to go to hospital and so he was stretchered into the back of the ambulance.

As it drove away, Hunter turned to his tutor. 'You obviously know him. Who is he?'

'That, young Kerr, is George Arthur Hudson. Jud Hudson to us. He is one elusive character who you will come up against on a regular basis if you stick around. Jud has convictions for most things and he's been in and out of the nick more times than I've had hot suppers. Believe me, if it's not nailed down, Jud will nick it.'

'So, are we going to search for evidence then?'

'Evidence?'

'Yeah. See if he's been trying to rip the lead off the roof.'

Roger looked up the side of the outbuilding. 'And you're willing to risk your neck going up there to search, are you?'

Hunter met his tutor's gaze and pursed his lips.

Roger shook his head. 'I think it would be fair to say some summary justice has been dished out tonight. Let's leave it at that. There will always be another time for Jud.'

Following his seven days on the graveyard shift, as he'd learned it was called, Hunter spent most of his two days off catching up on much needed sleep. When he was awake, he spent most of his time lying on his bed reading his law books, in preparation for his next student exam, or listening to his new Guns and Roses CD.

Mid-afternoon on the second day, he did manage to summon up the vigour to go down to his father's boxing academy, but after an hour of pushing weights and punching the bag, his energy levels were sapped, and he grabbed a shower, and then spent half an hour with his dad, over a mug of tea, telling him snippets from his night duty, particularly the incident with Jud Hudson at The Drum.

It brought a chuckle from his father, who told him that he had heard of Jud from some of the boxers he coached, though he'd never had an encounter with him himself, and promised to keep an ear out for him if ever his name was mentioned.

Hunter was especially close to his dad, spending a lot of time training, sparring and being coached by him, and normally told him everything, but on this occasion, he deliberately chose not to tell him about the practical joke that had been played on him because he was still feeling humiliated.

As Hunter lay in bed that night with the bedside light on, eyes resting on his pressed uniform hanging from the wardrobe door and polished boots below, he thought about the week that had gone and hoped that his final week with his tutor would bring about something more exciting.

CHAPTER THREE

The following afternoon, Roger Mills held open the door to the rear station yard, and as Hunter slipped past, he handed him a piece of paper containing a scribbled down address.

'The sergeant's just given me that,' Roger told Hunter. 'A call came in an hour ago about concern for an elderly lady who hasn't been seen for a week. This could be your first sudden death.'

Hunter glanced at the address and as he made his way to the beat car his thoughts went into a spin. He'd never seen a dead body before, especially one which might have been dead for some time, and his brain was beginning to conjure up awful images from films he'd seen.

Fifteen minutes later, Hunter and Roger were looking up and down the frontage of 32 Mexborough Row. It was an end-terrace house and it had all the looks of years of neglect. Green paint peeled from the windows and doors and stained and faded white nets failed to hide the grimy windows.

Roger twisted the front door handle.

'We've already tried that, love.' A busty middle-aged woman appeared at their side. 'And we couldn't check the back, 'cause the gates locked and the wall's too high to see over.'

'Are you the person who rung us up?' asked Roger.

She nodded, folding her arms, supporting her large bust. 'I haven't seen June for the best part of a week. Haven't even heard her with the telly on. I'm her neighbour.' She dipped her head behind her to number 30, where the front door was open.

'Is that unusual?'

'With June it is. She's got a bit of a drink problem, has our June, and keeps strange hours. We don't see much of her during the day, but you can hear her most nights with her telly or music blaring out. Not all the time, to be fair, but some nights are louder than others, and Gary — that's my hubby — has to bang on the wall to get her to turn it down. This last week, we haven't heard a peep from her, and I got a bit worried last night, so I've knocked on her door several times this morning but got no answer.'

'You wouldn't happen to know if she's any family nearby, would you?' asked Roger.

The busty woman shook her head. 'None as far as I'm aware. She's certainly got no kids. She told me years ago she was once married, but her hubby was gone before me and Gary came to live here, and we've been here nearly thirty years. She's had a few men staying with her over the years, but none of them serious, as you would say. The longest any of them stayed was about six months.

'I don't want to put June down, but the blokes she bought home were just as bad as she was when it came to drink. We used to hear some shocking rows through the walls. And we know some of them used to knock her about, but June could certainly give as much as she took. Except for the last one. The last one gave her a right hiding. She ended up in hospital. Dean was his name. Don't know his second name. You locked him up. That was roughly nine months ago now.'

Roger acknowledged her comments with a nod. 'No one staying with her since?'

The neighbour shook her head. 'She's kept herself to herself since then. To be honest, she blames us for calling you lot, so except for saying hello, we have very little to do with her now. Me and Gary are at work Monday to Friday, so other than hearing her TV or music at night, that's the only thing we hear from her. As I say, we've not heard anything from her all this week.'

Roger thanked the neighbour with a courteous nod and switched his gaze to Hunter. 'Come on then, let's see if we can find a way in.'

The rear of the property was surrounded by a six-foot wall, and as the neighbour had explained, the rear gate was locked, so Hunter had to help Roger with a foothold over and then scramble up himself to get into the back yard. The yard was overgrown with weeds poking through hundreds of cracks in the concrete. A decrepit faux leather settee rested against an outhouse and a broken television lay next to it.

Roger made for the back door. Turning the handle, he pushed against it but it was locked. He tried again, this time with more force. It hardly moved. The third time, Roger slammed all of his 14 stone against it but failed to shift it from its frame.

'Fuck me, that door's like Fort Knox,' he said, rubbing his shoulder. 'There's nothing else for it, Hunter, we'll have to break a window and you'll have to climb in and open it.'

Wrenching out his hasp, Hunter ratcheted it out to its full length, and with a deft swing, sharply smacked the corner of the lower rear window. Shards of glass exploded everywhere.

'Well, that was subtle,' Roger said with a smile. 'I bet they didn't teach you that at training school.'

'Did I do something wrong?' asked Hunter, throwing his tutor a puzzled look.

'Personally, I would have just given it a tap near the sash lock, but your method's had the desired effect. Carry on,' Roger replied, with a grin.

Knocking and scraping out the stubborn pieces from the wooden casement, Hunter carefully negotiated the hole he had made, pushed the net curtain to one side and began his climb through the window. He put out a hand to support himself, cursing in disgust as his hand slipped over a greasy kitchen sink.

He dropped inside the kitchen. A rancid smell immediately assaulted his nostrils and he cringed. Wiping his slimed hand on the net curtain, he scanned the dim room. The place was filthy. Dirty crockery covered the table and the floor was sticky and stained. He went to the back door, which he could see was bolted in several places. It was no wonder Roger couldn't move it, he thought. He pulled them back and tried the handle but it was still locked. He scoured the work surfaces and the table for a key, but there wasn't one.

He shouted back his findings to Roger.

'In that case have a look round. See if you can see anything of June and if you need any help I'll come in the same way as you.'

'Thanks,' muttered Hunter, and he turned towards the front of the house.

He entered the front room cautiously. That was also dim, but he immediately saw it was unoccupied. He made for the staircase and as he lifted his face the stench from above hit him. It was a cloying, mainly a tepid urine smell, but it was strong and his stomach leaped to his throat. Gripping his nose and partially covering his mouth he climbed the stairs carefully.

On the landing, he paused. The overwhelming reek was coming from the bedroom to his right, which overlooked the front of the house. The door to it was slightly ajar, and taking a deep breath, he pushed it open further with the toe of his boot.

Hunter's first thought, as his eyes scanned the room, was how sparsely furnished it was. The only light came from a patch that streamed through a gap in the heavy velvet curtains and undulated across dozens of items of clothing that appeared to be dirty washing. Against one wall, he saw a large, solid looking, dark wood bed, covered in an array of stained bedding.

He made a step towards it. As he edged closer, he could feel his heart thumping against his chest. A couple of feet from the bed he spotted a head poking out of the sheets, resting on a pillow. It was an emaciated waxen face with dark rimmed sunken closed eyes. Several hopping flies attracted him to a small amount of dried blood that had spilled from the woman's nose onto her mouth.

Hunter had never seen anything like it and the gut-wrenching smell was shocking. Taking another quick look at the corpse, Hunter backed out of the room to get Roger.

As he neared the bottom of the stairs, Hunter spotted a key lying on the carpet by the front door and he picked it up and tried it in the lock. Flinging open the door, he took in a deep breath of fresh air.

Following Hunter's call, Roger clambered back over the wall and joined him at the front of the house.

His heart racing, Hunter explained what he had found.

Roger grasped him on the shoulder. 'Well, at least you've not thrown up everywhere.' Then, looking back into the house, he said, 'Come on then, let's have a look at we've got.'

Hunter threw his tutor a pleading look. 'Do I have to?'

A smirk broke across Roger's mouth. 'This is your job, kiddo. Welcome to my world.'

Hunter followed Roger back upstairs to the bedroom at the front, where the pair stood beside the bed, gazing down at the body.

'How long do you think she's been dead?' asked Hunter softly.

'She's probably been like this for the best of a week, but the stink is not all coming from her. The state of the house is causing most of it, and what you see in her face is down to the lifestyle she's led. She's in a surprisingly good state given how long she's probably been dead. I've seen a lot worse bodies than this one.'

'Do you think anything untoward's happened to her?'

'What? Tucked up like this?'

'I was thinking about the blood from her nose,' Hunter replied, pointing at the brown crusted deposit around her mouth.

Roger shook his head. 'She's a drinker, isn't she? That happens sometimes.' Roger scanned his eyes around the room. 'There's no sign of any bruising anywhere on her face, and how many killers leave their victims tucked up in bed? To my eyes, the state of this room is down to the way she lives, rather than it being ransacked by a burglar. And don't forget, the back door was locked and bolted, and the front door was also locked, and except for you busting the kitchen window, there's no sign of a break-in.'

Hunter acknowledged that with a nod.

'No, all things considered, I think you'll find this is just a normal sudden death. I bet the post mortem finds her liver and kidneys just couldn't take any more.' Roger returned his gaze to the woman's gaunt, yellow face and shook his head. 'Sad way to come to the end of your life, don't you think?'

Hunter thought about his tutor's words and without warning thoughts of Polly jumped inside his head. He wondered what she had looked like when they found her? A cold shiver travelled down his back.

'Anyway, we need to call the doctor out to give her the once over before he pronounces death. If he thinks there's anything suspicious, we can call out CID.'

Roger's words brought Hunter's thoughts back to the case in hand and he got on his radio.

After updating the control room, and while waiting for the on call doctor to arrive, Hunter and Roger made a cursory search of the house, for anything which would provide better identification than the name June, which the neighbour had provided. They both put on their leather gloves for the search — the place was a hovel. Each of the rooms were filthy — they looked as though they hadn't been cleaned for years — with empty litre bottles of cider and empty cans of high-strength lager lying around on every surface, interspersed with dirty takeaway cartons and the odd stained mug of furred-over coffee.

By the time they got into the lounge, Hunter had got used to the smell. He targeted a sideboard to search, while Roger made for a set of drawers next to the fireplace, on which was perched a small portable TV.

Hunter opened the first drawer. It was full of household bills — just what he was looking for. He pulled out a bundle, sifted through and picked out the council tax bill. 'June Waring,' he mumbled as he read the details.

'What did you say?' Roger called back.

Hunter turned to his tutor. 'Her name's June Waring,' he responded, waving the council tax document.

'Good start, Hunter. See if you can find a birth certificate for her, or her marriage certificate. The neighbour said she thought she'd been married. I'm sure she'll not have a passport or driving licence.'

Hunter nodded and returned to the task of searching the sideboard.

Ten minutes later, in the last of three drawers, he found what he had been looking for — a marriage certificate. He read over the details, before turning to Roger, holding up the certificate. 'Guess how old June was?'

'Early to mid-70s?'

'I'd have said the same looking at her but according to her marriage certificate she was only 61.'

'Bloody hell, she has had a rough life.' Roger shook his head. 'That's what drink does for you.'

'She was born in 1940. She married a Graham Chappell in 1961 at Doncaster Register Office.'

'Well, that's a good start.'

Following that discovery, Roger joined Hunter, and the pair continued to search the sideboard, upon which they found June Waring's birth certificate, revealing she had been born in the nearby town of Mexborough, and they also discovered paperwork revealing her divorce to Graham Chappell in 1964. There were no documents to suggest she had ever remarried.

'This paperwork will help you when you do her death report. All you need to add is the result from her post mortem, and try and track down the last person who saw her, and that's it, your first sudden death,' said Roger. Following a pause, he added, 'Not difficult, is it?'

'Sad though, eh?' Hunter responded, flicking his head ceiling-bound in the direction of June Waring's bedroom.

'Well, it is, but just store what you've seen today, and what's caused it, and don't let yourself go down the same route. Life is valuable, young Kerr, so live it.'

It was another hour before the on call doctor got there. Dr Raj carried out a brief examination of the body, answering Hunter's query about the nosebleed by explaining that it had more than likely occurred following a heart attack and then left them to it.

It was another hour of waiting around for the undertakers to come to take away June's body and it was almost 7 pm before they got back to the station, and for the remainder of the shift Roger helped Hunter make a start on the Sudden Death Report for June Waring.

By the time 10 pm came around — the end of afternoon shift — Hunter was ready for a beer, and together with most of the group, made his way to the Kings Head pub, a stone's throw from the police station and a regular haunt for the cops after finishing their shift.

It was almost midnight by the time Hunter got home. No lights were on as he entered his home — his parents had gone to bed. He made his way upstairs and confined his uniform shirt and trousers to the wash basket, swearing he could still smell the stench of June's decaying body and disgusting house on them, and then, slinging on his dressing gown, he soft-footed to the bathroom and grabbed a warmer than normal shower, before tucking himself up in bed.

As he lay in the dark, his brain on overdrive, stark images of June Waring's withered face jumped inside his head and rummaged around on rewind, keeping him awake.

CHAPTER FOUR

Stepping outside the hospital mortuary, gently letting the door close behind him, Hunter took in a great gulp of fresh air and shuddered. What he had just experienced would stay with him for the rest of his life. Roger had warned him what to expect from a post-mortem, but his imagination hadn't prepared him for the real horror, especially when he had seen the scalp and face of Jane Waring being peeled down to reveal her glistening white skull.

The sight had taken him by surprise and had made him feel light-headed. He'd only stopped his legs buckling beneath him by grasping hold of the metal sink he was standing next to. What had been even worse was the sound of the oscillating saw cutting the cap off the skull.

And that smell. It was worse than when he had first discovered her body. He pulled up the collar of his jacket and sniffed. It was still there, impregnated into the blue serge. He shuddered again.

But it wasn't just the sight and smell that had shocked him, but also the surprise revelation from the pathologist once he had sliced open Jane Waring's chest and cut out her heart.

Hunter made the personal radio call to Roger.

Before he had time to say anything, Roger said, 'All done, Hunter, need picking up?'

'Yes, err, yes,' he stammered over his words, and then added, 'But it's not a straightforward death, Roger.'

Roger instantly came back on the air. 'What do you mean it's not straightforward?'

'She's been murdered,' Hunter replied. 'June's been murdered.'

'Hang on there, kiddo, I'm going to get hold of CID. We'll be with you in twenty minutes.'

Roger turned up in the panda car less than half an hour later with DC John Vickers in the front seat. As John Vickers pulled himself out of the car Hunter cast his eyes upon him. He was a couple inches taller than him and more solid and Hunter guessed he was in his mid-40s. He had sandy, greying hair, and was slightly overweight, with a beer belly, and was dressed in a navy-blue blazer, white shirt, blue and grey striped kipper tie, and grey slacks.

'Roger has filled me in about yesterday,' John Vickers said, 'and it seems that at the time there was nothing to suggest anything suspicious about the death. Is that right?'

Hunter was unsure how to respond. It felt as though he was being quizzed by the detective. Swallowing the lump in his throat, he answered, 'Well, yes.'

John nodded, his lips pursing. 'And the pathologist is saying it isn't a natural death?'

Hunter nodded sharply. 'Yeah. He says she died of a heart attack brought on by stress. He's also done a thorough examination and says there are signs of sexual violence with extensive bruising to her vagina and anus, and there is slight bruising to her wrists that is very recent.'

'What?' Both Roger and John expressed their surprise at the same time.

Hunter nodded again.

'Run past me exactly what the pathologist has said, will you?' said John.

Hunter looked at the notes he had made and then engaged eyes with John Vickers.

'When he first examined her, he said he suspected it was a heart attack, but when he cut open her heart, he confirmed it had been caused by stress. He said that stress on the heart damages muscle and releases a cardiac enzyme that can be instantly recognised, and that in this case there were all the signs that June Waring's heart had suffered extreme stress. He said he needed some further tests to be done regarding the levels of the enzyme in her blood, but he suspected, looking at the condition of the damage to heart, that it will be pretty high. That's when he carried out a more thorough examination and found the injuries to her vagina and anus.

'He also found bruising to the inside of her nose, and is of the opinion that was caused by having her head forced face-down into the bed whilst she was being anally raped.' He switched his gaze from John to Roger. 'That's how she would have got her nosebleed.' Following a short pause, he added, 'The pathologist has also found bruising to her wrists, and is of the opinion her rapist grabbed hold of her wrists and pinned her down before raping her.'

'Jesus,' John Vickers exclaimed.

'The pathologist's taken swabs for DNA comparison,' Hunter told them.

John Vickers turned to Roger and said, 'But I thought you said that there was no sign of a struggle. That you found her tucked up in bed?'

Roger's mouth set tight. 'We did. She was laid flat on back with the covers pulled up to her chin.' He sought out Hunter's support.

Hunter responded with a curt nod.

'And there was no sign of any break-in?'

'None.' Roger shook his head as he answered. 'The back door was locked and bolted and the front door was locked. Hunter found the key to the front door lying on the carpet in the hallway. The house was in quite a bad state, from the way June lived, but it didn't look as though the place had been searched or ransacked.'

John Vickers looked at Hunter. 'Is the pathologist still here?'

Hunter nodded. 'Yes. He said he had another PM to do and then he'll write up his report before he finishes for the day.'

'Good. I want a quick word with him. You two hang on here a couple of minutes and then we'll drive over to June Waring's house and have a look-see.'

After John Vickers went inside the mortuary, Hunter turned to Roger and said, 'Have we done something wrong?'

'No, why?'

'Just the way John was questioning us.'

'No, John's just being thorough. You'll soon find that some in CID think they're a cut above us woodentops but John is not one of them. I've had a few jobs with him and he's sound.'

'Oh, good, 'cause I thought we'd done a pretty good job.'

'We did, don't worry.'

At that, the door of the mortuary flew open, interrupting their conversation.

John Vickers strode through. 'Right, lads, I've got things fixed in my head. Let's get back to the station, pick up the key for June Waring's house, and I'll fill my sergeant in and then we'll shoot up to her place.'

CHAPTER FIVE

'Fuck me, what a smell,' said John, pushing open the front door of 32 Mexborough Row.

'We had five hours of this yesterday,' Roger replied, following the detective into the hallway.

John stopped by the stairway, casting his eyes around the hall. 'So, you said the front door was locked, as well as the back door and so you had to break in by the back window?'

'Yes, the kitchen window,' Roger responded, pointing over the detective's shoulder. 'Hunter climbed in and went upstairs and found her dead, and then called me and let me in by the front door.'

'I couldn't open the back door — it was bolted and I couldn't find the key,' Hunter interjected.

'And you say you found the front door key here, in the hallway?' said John.

Hunter nodded. 'I didn't notice it at first. I had a quick look in the front room and then went upstairs. After I saw that she was dead, I came downstairs and spotted the key on the carpet, by the front door.'

'Close to it?'

Hunter looked at him, puzzled. 'Pretty close. About a foot from it.'

John returned a quick nod and walked into the kitchen, stopping just inside. 'Bloody hell, this is a fucking shit hole,' he said, looking around.

'The rest of the house is no different,' returned Roger.

'No wonder you said it didn't look as though there'd been a break-in. If the rest of the house is bad as this, you wouldn't be able to tell if there'd been a burglary here or not. And I wouldn't have thought there was anything worth nicking anyway.' John gave the kitchen another quick look-over, and then returned to the hallway and started climbing the stairs. 'Which bedroom did you find her body in?' he asked, over his shoulder.

'The front one,' Hunter and Roger replied in unison, following the detective up the stairs.

There was more light streaming in the bedroom now — Hunter had opened the curtains yesterday to allow the on call doctor to get a better look at June when he examined her — and it exposed just how dirty and untidy the room was. Hunter could now see half a dozen empty cider bottles beneath the bed that he hadn't noticed before, and the bedding was even grubbier in the afternoon sun. He felt a shudder down his back. How on earth could someone live like this?

'And you say June was tucked up in bed, as if she was asleep?' John asked, staring at the stained, dishevelled bedding.

'She was laid on her back under the sheets and the top throw was pulled up to her chin. All you could see was her face — nothing else,' Roger replied.

John gave an understanding nod and scoured the bedroom. 'What was she wearing?' he asked, resting his eyes on the bed, the grubby sheets of which were pulled back to reveal a stained mattress.

'Just a t-shirt,' Hunter replied.

'Any underwear?'

Hunter thought about it for a moment and then shook his head. 'No. When the undertaker took her away all she had on was the t-shirt. It was manky, all stained, like she hadn't got changed to go to bed.'

John nodded again. 'This is one cool cucumber, I'll give him that, getting into her house, raping her, and covering it up by tucking her up in bed, to make it look like she's just had a heart attack and died.'

'How do you think he got in?' Hunter asked.

'That I'm not sure,' John replied, shrugging his shoulders. 'But you said there was no sign of a struggle downstairs.' Pursing his lips, he continued, 'Maybe she was already in bed. And given the drunken state she's usually in, she wouldn't have given any thought about locking up. Could be that whoever did this knew that and let himself in.'

'So you think it's someone who knew June then?'

'Probably someone who knew what her regular habits were, or the state she was usually in. Wouldn't be that hard, given the type of person she was and the lifestyle she led,' John responded, stroking his chin. 'Could be someone on this street, or it could be anyone from any one of the boozers she drank in. I'm keeping an open mind until I've made some enquiries. One thing I am certain of is that whoever did this has made a good attempt at trying to cover it up, even locking up after and posting the key through the door. If the pathologist hadn't been on the ball, this guy would have got away with it.' He gave another look around the room, rubbing his hands together. 'Right, Roger, I need you to give me a lift back to the station. I'm going to update my sergeant, and get some more bodies back here to start doing some house-to-house, and I need to get hold of Scenes of Crime.' He looked at Hunter. 'I want you to guard the scene by the front door, and don't let anyone in here until I get back, understand?'

Hunter nodded sharply.

'Oh, and just one more question — did you two touch much in the house?'

'You'll find my prints on the glass where I broke in through the kitchen window and on the work surface near the kitchen sink,' Hunter replied, feeling embarrassed, given that the house was now a murder scene. 'I didn't touch anything going upstairs, and her bedroom door was open, so I didn't touch that, and when me and Roger were searching for some identification, after I found her dead, we both wore our gloves.'

'That's good.'

'Oh, I've just realised I picked the key up and turned the handle of the front door to let Roger in,' Hunter added. 'I'm sorry.'

John took a step towards the door. 'Never mind, can't be helped. Given what you've told me, you weren't to know there was anything suspicious about her death.'

It was almost two hours before John Vickers returned and he was without Roger. Instead, he was driving a CID car, and with him was DC David Allen, whom Hunter had seen around the station, but had never had cause to speak with before now.

By this time Hunter was bored. The neighbour had been out to question him about what was going off, and he'd fended her off with the response that they weren't happy with how June had died and further enquiries were being done. It wasn't an honest answer, he knew, but he hadn't been left instructions on what he could or couldn't say and wasn't sure how much he could disclose right now. What he had told the woman seemed to placate her and she'd offered him a biscuit with a mug of tea.

'Anything happened, or anybody been round, since I left?' asked John.

'Only the neighbour.'

'You say anything to her?'

Hunter told John what he had said.

'Good man. You're learning. It'll soon get out after tonight, but you still don't need to give anything away for now.'

Hunter acknowledged this with a nod.

John handed him a clipboard with some paperwork attached. 'Right, young man, that's the log. Your job is to write down everyone who goes inside the house. But, and this is a big but, the only people who go in there are SOCO and me, and anyone else who's with me. And the only person that will be is my gaffer. You got that?'

Hunter responded with a nod.

'And if anyone asks you anything, you stick to what you've told the neighbour. And if it's the press, you don't even tell them that. You refer them to me. Yes?'

'Yes.'

John tapped Hunter on the shoulder. 'Good man. We'll make a copper out of you yet.' Then, looking around, he said, 'Me and Dave here are going to start knocking on some doors. The moment SOCO arrive get me on my radio. Okay?'

Hunter nodded again, and watched John and Dave head next door, starting their enquiries with the neighbour. He wished it was him going in that house instead of being left bored to death on his own.

It was 10.30 before Hunter's relief arrived — half an hour past the end of his shift. DC John Vickers and his sidekick, Dave Allen, had driven away 90 minutes earlier, together with the Scenes of Crime Officer, telling Hunter that they were going back to brief the DI and he was to hold the fort until he was relieved of duty.

By the time Hunter got back to the station, he was cold and frustrated. To cap it all, his team had all gone and, disappointed that no one had waited for him, he caught the bus home feeling totally deflated.

The moment Hunter stepped through the kitchen door his dad, who was making a pot of tea, greeted him with, 'We've seen you on the local news tonight, son. It said you're investigating a suspicious death of a woman on Mexborough Row.'

Hunter suddenly remembered the estate car that had stopped opposite June Waring's house hours ago and the man in the padded coat getting out with his camera. The man hadn't stayed long, or approached him, before driving off again, and Hunter was surprised the case had already been aired on the news.

'What did it say?' Hunter asked, slipping off his jacket and draping it over the back of one of the chairs around the kitchen table.

At this point his mother, Fiona, appeared in her dressing gown.

Jock set out three cups for them and then replied, 'Nothing much at all. I don't think it was on for even a minute. They just showed you guarding the house — you looked very smart, by the way — and said that police were investigating a suspicious death there and then they showed a couple of forensics people going in. That was it.'

'Did they mention her name?'

Jock shook his head. 'No. They just said an elderly woman died at the address. Why — is it someone we know?'

'No. Her name's June Waring. I've never come across her and I can't remember seeing her around town before.'

'Has she been attacked or something?' asked Fiona, in her soft Scottish accent. Whereas Jock's Scottish accent was still broad, Fiona's had flattened and softened in the 18 years she had been living in Yorkshire.

Jock and Fiona had been born and bred on the eastern fringes of Glasgow, where things had been harsh, but Jock had managed to eke out a life for them as a boxer until injury had brought an end to his career at the tender age of 21.

Hunter had just been six months old at the time, and Jock had made the decision to launch a new career as a boxing coach, finding suitable premises in Barnwell, where he'd relocated and started his own boxing academy. Jock had made a success of it — the academy turning out some good young prospects — and it had given them a good quality of life.

Hunter thought about what John Vickers had said to him and answered, 'I've been told not to say anything at the moment.'

Fiona cocked her head and gave him one of her looks. Still holding his gaze, she said, 'Well, you sit yourself down —' stepping towards the fridge — 'I'll get you a sandwich. You must be starved, stood outside that house all night.'

Jock said, 'But, we're your parents, son, we're not going to go about blethering to folk what you're up to. Can't you tell us anything at all? You know we're interested in what you do.'

Pulling off one boot, Hunter replied, 'Look, you need to keep this to yourself. I could get in very serious trouble if this comes out before it's on the news or in the papers.'

His mother relaxed her stare and touched her lips with the tip of her fingers, indicating they would remain sealed.

Jock nodded.

Slipping off his other boot, Hunter told them that it was suspected June Waring had been raped and had died from a heart attack as a result. He didn't tell them about her gruesome autopsy.

'So, you're dealing with her murder then, son?' said Jock.

Hunter smiled. 'Not me, Dad. It's CID that do that. I just had to look after the house while it was being examined by Scenes of Crime for forensics.'

'But that's still an important job, son.'

Hunter's smile got wider. 'Yes, I guess it is.'

Finishing his ham sandwich and mug of tea, Hunter bid his parents goodnight and retired to bed, once more confining his shirt and trousers to the wash basket because it smelt as if they were impregnated with the stench from the mortuary.

As he pulled on a pair of shorts ready for bed, Polly popped into his thoughts. He cringed at the thought that she'd undergone the same treatment from a pathologist as June had following her murder. He tried to dismiss the thought by squeezing shut his eyes, willing himself to go to sleep but it didn't work.

Hunter knew it was going to be another sleepless night.

CHAPTER SIX

'You've got in early. What are you up to?'

At the sound of Roger's voice, Hunter stopped typing and looked up. 'John Vickers rang me at home first thing this morning. He wanted me to get the Sudden Death Report done for June Waring, so I came in at 12.'

'And how's it going?'

'Just putting in the info from her post-mortem, and then it's done, I think. Will you check through it to see that I've put in everything I need to before it goes upstairs?'

Hunter was referring to the CID Department situated on the upper floor of the two-storey 1970s red-brick station; downstairs was where uniform were based, housing the parade room, report writing room, inspector's office, cell area and interview room, and upstairs, alongside the district superintendent and admin, were CID and Stolen Vehicle Squad.

Leaning over Hunter's shoulder to get a glimpse of the report on the screen, Roger said, 'Did much happen after I left yesterday?'

Hunter shook his head. 'John came back with Dave Allen, and they did a couple of enquiries with the neighbours, and SOCO came. Other than that, nothing.' Following a pause, he said, 'What happened to you?'

'Had my meal and then went back out on patrol. They said they didn't need me anymore. Just asked me to do my statement today.'

'So is that it then? No more enquiries?'

'For us it is, kiddo. The only time we'll hear anything now is when they lock up who's done it.'

'That's crap.'

'That's the job for you. We get all the shit jobs and CID get all the glory. You'll get used to it.' Roger rested a hand on Hunter's shoulder. 'Finish your report off and write up your pocket book while I'm doing my statement and then, after briefing, you can do your statement before we go out.'

Hunter nodded and returned his eyes to the monitor.

Hunter was putting the finishing touches to the evidence in his pocketbook when Roger burst into the report writing room, making him jump.

'Come on, Hunter, get your stuff, we've got a domestic to go to on Woodland Road,' he said and scurried back out again.

Hunter jammed his pocket book into his coat pocket, snatched up his belt containing his hasp and handcuffs and bolted towards the back door. He found Roger revving the engine of the marked response car, ready to go. Leaping into the front passenger seat, Hunter hadn't even belted up before the Ford Sierra was tearing out of the rear yard towards the Tree Estate.

'We've had several calls that a man and woman are fighting,' Roger said, switching on the siren.

In less than ten minutes they were speeding onto Woodland Road and seconds later Roger braked sharply before the scene which confronted them: a throng of shouting and excited people were enveloping one of the gardens halfway along the street.

Roger pulled the car sharply into the side of the road, switched off the blues-and-twos and sprang open his door.

Hunter followed, fastening his hasp and cuff belt around his waist as he stepped to back up his partner.

Above the shouts of the bystanders were the screams of a woman, so loud, as they approached at a jog, that Hunter was convinced someone was being murdered. Suddenly, he could feel the adrenalin beginning its rush inside his brain and his stomach lurched.

As they pushed their way through the midst of spectators they were greeted by shouts of disgust in their direction, but no resistance was offered, and as they squeezed past the front row they were confronted by a shaven-headed, middle-aged man who was straddling a spread-eagled woman of similar age. The man held a handful of hair, the colour of which was debateable — the blonde parts definitely from a bottle — while the woman thrashed around, beating and scratching at the man's bare arms. Both were so heavily tattooed that it was difficult to determine who displayed the most designs.

'Alice, Jack, pack it in,' shouted Roger, moving into the fray and trying his best to grab one set of flying hands.

A final punch was flung, connecting with the woman's right eye and her head flew back into the overgrown garden. The blow laid her motionless for several seconds, giving Roger the space to restrain the man.

'I'll kill the unfaithful fucking bitch!' the man shouted as Roger secured a grip on the man's wrists.

Hunter bent down to assist the woman who was beginning to come around. In less than a minute he had his hands under her armpits and was helping her up.

Roger was manhandling the man through the front door of the house, shouting back over his shoulder, 'Everyone back to your homes — performance over!'

Hunter followed in his partner's wake, supporting the woman into the hallway. As he kicked shut the door the woman flung herself free and darted claw-like fingers in the direction of the man's face.

She screamed, 'You bastard!'

Recovering quickly, Hunter locked his arms around the woman's waist and wrestled her through a doorway into the lounge. There, he could restrain her no longer and found himself tumbling onto the sofa, she falling on top. For a few seconds he wriggled beneath her until finally he squirmed himself free.

She pushed herself up.

Hunter latched onto the hateful stare she threw him.

Adjusting her upper clothing, she lashed out, 'Don't you get fresh with me, young man, I'm old enough to be your mother.'

Hunter exchanged glances with Roger, who was ushering in the shaven-headed man, one hand still firmly clasping the shoulder of his t-shirt. A smirk was plastered all over Roger's face.

The woman started finger-wagging — aiming her digit spear-like in the direction of the dishevelled man. 'I want him arrested. Look at this eye. You saw what he did. I've 100 witnesses out there. I want him locked up this time.'

Roger stepped in front, twisting the man around. 'Alice, will you calm down just a minute?'

The woman withdrew, defensively folding her arms. 'There's no need to shout, I'm not bloody deaf.'

'We have this every time, Alice. How many times have I been here and locked your Jack up?' He paused and searched her face. 'Must have been at least a dozen times. And what happens every time — you withdraw your complaint. We can't carry on like this.'

'Well, I've really had enough this time. He's never blacked my eye before. Next time you'll find me dead. I want him arrested.'

Throughout Alice's berating, Hunter had been carefully observing the woman's husband. His face had a forlorn look.

'If I arrest him, Alice,' Roger continued, 'it'll mean taking statements and airing all your dirty washing in court.'

'I don't care this time. He should be locked up.'

Roger turned and faced Jack.

Jack said, 'She's been shagging a mate of mine. Well, I thought he was a mate. He's not any fucking more.'

Roger shrugged his shoulders. He glanced back at Alice. She displayed a brazen look. Returning to his prisoner he said, 'Sorry Jack, I can't appease her. It's the nick, I'm afraid.'

Jack straightened himself. 'You'll have to handcuff me, Mr Mills. I'm not going out in the chuffing streets without them. I've got a reputation to keep up.'

For a few seconds Roger stared at Jack, then he said, 'Okay, if that's the way you want it.' He produced his handcuffs and clicked them around the man's outstretched wrists. He made a check they weren't nipping and then took hold of his arm.

Hunter was about to take hold of Jack's other arm when he caught a sharp movement at the periphery of his vision. Without warning, a shiny red high-heeled shoe flashed past his nose and struck Jack to the side of his head. A faint cry issued from Jack's mouth and his legs buckled, dropping him to the floor with a thud.

Hunter spun around to meet a delighted-looking Alice, dropping her other shoe.

'I don't want to complain now,' she announced, picking up the TV remote, switching it on and flopping into an armchair. 'And neither will he, because if folk find out I've done that he'll be a right bloody laughing stock.' She crossed her legs. 'There's no need to wait while he comes around. He'll be okay. You can take your cuffs off him now and piss off.'

Hunter looked down at the shaven-headed man lying prostrate with blood pouring from his head, then turned his gaze to his partner. This was unlike any scenario he had faced during training school.

Roger again shrugged his shoulders, reached down and unlocked the handcuffs on Jack who was beginning to come around. Blood was now trickling onto the carpet from a deep gash at his temple.

Flicking his head at Hunter, Roger said, 'I'm going to call for an ambulance. You make sure these two don't go round two with one another.'

It took the ambulance ten minutes to get to them. In that time, Roger had got the first aid kit from the boot of the car and wrapped a temporary bandage around Jack's head.

At first, Jack refused to go to hospital, but when one of the paramedics removed the bandage to get a look, and blood started pouring again, he changed his mind.

Hunter and Roger watched Jack being helped into the ambulance and followed after it as it made its way to Barnwell General Hospital. As they pulled onto the main road in the direction of the hospital, Hunter said, 'You obviously know those two?'

With his eyes firmly on the ambulance in front, Roger replied, 'That man is Jack Paynton, and his wife is Alice Paynton. You remember what I said about Jud Hudson the other day? Well those two are on a par. You can bet a pound to a pinch of shit you'll come across them again. And they've got two young tearaway sons as well. The whole family are a pain in the arse.' He chinned towards the ambulance. 'All we are going to do is make sure Jack is all right, make sure he doesn't want to make a complaint, which he won't, and then we leave.'

'But we saw Alice hit him with her shoe,' Hunter responded.

Roger shot his head sideways and snapped, 'We saw nothing of the sort. Savvy?' and returned his gaze to the road in front.

Hunter quickly took in his mentor's response and slowly answered, 'Okay.'

'There are times when it's prudent to turn a blind eye, and this is one of those times. We just make sure he's going to be okay and then we leave him. We've got some real police work to do.'

At Barnwell General Hospital, Hunter booked in Jack Paynton with a stern-faced receptionist, while Roger had a word with one of the nurses about their patient. It resulted in them being immediately whisked away to a cubicle, where Roger left Hunter, telling him to look after Jack, while he went and got a cuppa.

Behind the curtains, Jack was surprisingly quiet and Hunter put it down to him being embarrassed at what Alice had done to him; he had already gathered from Roger that Alice had been on the end of quite a number of beatings by Jack, and this is probably the first time she had managed to turn the tables on him. All Hunter could think was that this had served him right and it might make Jack think twice in future.

Twenty minutes later a young female doctor arrived. She began unwinding the strapping the paramedics had treated Jack's head wound with. The last strip was stuck to his wound by dried blood and he winced as the doctor pulled it away.

'Fucking hell!' Jack cried, rearing up.

The doctor jumped back and Hunter quickly stepped in, pushing Jack down on the bed by his shoulder. 'Just you be careful, Jack,' Hunter said sternly. 'You're already lucky not to be getting locked up.'

'Well, it fucking hurt, that.'

'She's only doing her job.' Hunter stepped aside again to let the doctor look at the wound.

'How did you do this?' the doctor asked, smoothing a gloved hand along the edge of the dark bloodied hole, close to Jack's temple.

'His wife hit him with her stiletto shoe,' Hunter interjected, hiding a smirk.

'Fucking bitch,' Jack growled.

'Now that's enough, Jack,' Hunter reacted. 'Swear once more and I'm arresting you.'

'Well, she is,' he mumbled back.

'This is going to need a couple of sutures,' said the doctor, stepping back and peeling off her gloves. 'I'll get the nurse to come through and clean the wound up and give you a tetanus jab.' With that she swished aside the curtain and disappeared.

Hunter was so tuned in to what was going on in the cubicles either side of them that he never heard the nurse approach, only becoming aware of her when the curtain parted. Instantly his eyes were drawn to her slim figure and pretty face. She had natural straw-blonde hair, which was tied up in a ponytail, and a flawless blue gaze, and when she offered him a friendly smile that radiated warmth, he was immediately captivated by her. The first thought that entered his head was, *gorgeous*, and he couldn't stop his face lighting up.

'Now this is worth getting beat up for,' said Jack, pushing himself up the bed, his gaze transfixed on the young nurse, who was holding out a tray with a syringe.

'You've already been warned, Jack,' Hunter responded in a deep tone. 'I won't tell you again.'

Without batting an eyelid, the young nurse set down the tray with the syringe and said, 'The doctor's just asked me to clean your wound up and give you a tetanus before she stitches it up.'

As she picked up the syringe Hunter caught sight of her name badge. Student Nurse Jones, he read. He lifted his gaze to her face and his mind suddenly became a void.

'You're going to feel just a little prick.'

Hunter couldn't resist responding with, 'Yes, he is.'

She turned her head and they locked eyes. He could see she was fighting back the urge to laugh.

Straightening her mouth and returning her gaze to her patient, she tested the syringe, squirting a little of the tetanus through the needle, and then leaned forward to give the injection.

'Very funny, the pair of you,' Jack said.

Stitched up and bandaged, Hunter led Jack Paynton out of A & E where Roger was waiting for them in the car. Helping him into the back of the response car, Hunter made sure Jack was belted up and then jumped into the front passenger seat.

'Are we good to go?' Roger asked, putting the car into gear.

'Very.'

'Right, we'll get this pillock home to his lovely wife, then and get off to the pub. I think we've earned a beer today, kiddo.'

Hunter returned a huge smile. He felt elated. Not only had he seen a wife-beater get a taste of his own medicine, he had also come away with Student Nurse Beth Jones's home number. It had been a very successful day.

CHAPTER SEVEN

Hunter plink-plonked the keyboard of the word processor, using a two finger system that he felt was increasing in speed with each report he tackled. He had spent the last hour and a half working through his statement for the CID investigation into the murder of June Waring and was just bringing it to a conclusion.

'Shall I get a bucket of water? That keyboard'll catch fire if you go any quicker.'

Hunter looked back to see PC Andy Sharpe leaning against a filing cabinet. 'You know what they say about sarcasm,' Hunter responded.

'What are you doing?'

Hunter explained.

'Rape and murder in your first six weeks! Not bad going that, Hunter. Some cops don't even get to be involved in one of those in their 30 years.'

'I only wish I could have been involved more.'

'Afraid only the CID boys get those jobs. A couple of years, and if you're still interested, you can give it a shot as an aid.' Andy pushed himself upright. 'Anyway, how long you gonna be?'

Hunter returned a curious look. 'A couple of minutes. I've just got to read through it and then sign it and get it upstairs to the incident room. Why?'

'You're teamed up with me this afternoon. Roger's got his appraisal with the inspector. I thought we'd go out and do some real police work — catch a few villains.'

'You bet.' Hunter scanned a quick eye over his closing paragraph and hit the print button. 'Give me ten minutes. I'll get this upstairs and then get my stuff.'

'Okay. I'll be outside in the car.'

Hunter strolled across the rear yard, carrying his helmet and gloves and with his overcoat draped over his arm. The arrival of autumn had brought in colder than average temperatures these past couple of days — weather he wasn't used to being out in at all hours of the day — and he was glad that the Tailoring Department had provided him with one of the new lined gaberdines when he had been kitted out for his uniform; some of his colleagues hadn't been issued with theirs yet and were mighty envious.

As he approached the patrol car, he caught sight of Andy Sharp admiring himself in the interior mirror and Hunter smirked to himself. This was typical of Andy — Roger regularly ribbed him that he couldn't pass a mirror without checking himself, which he would always rise to by swearing, or giving Roger the finger.

With five years service, Andy was completely different to Roger — an excitable character with a witty sense of humour. Yet at the same time, he was one of the keenest in the team, and his pursuance of offenders, especially of those who broke traffic laws, was infallibly consistent. Andy was also one of the best driver's Hunter had sat in with; he had been Andy's front seat passenger during three emergency situations since his arrival and Andy's handling of a car at hair-raising speeds was second to none.

Hunter had commented on this on all three occasions and Andy had confided in Hunter that all he wanted from his career was to be a member of Road Traffic.

Hunter pulled open the back door and threw in his helmet and overcoat.

Andy reset the interior mirror, raked his fingers through his mane of fair hair and said, 'All sorted then?' as he started the car.

Hunter nodded and jumped into the front.

With a screech of tyres, they sped out of the station yard.

Andy had pulled into a layby on a section of long, winding back road, leading to junction 35 of the A1, where for the last 20 minutes, he and Hunter had completed their document production books, following two hours of stopping and checking cars.

All afternoon drifting dark clouds had threatened rain and now a drizzle had started, peppering the windscreen and diminishing the view.

Andy had just flipped on the wipers when a screaming car flew shot past them, rocking the panda as it passed.

Hunter shot forward, just in time to see the brake lights flash on a gold Ford Escort Ghia as it disappeared round a sharp bend. He snapped his head sideways and caught the frown creasing Andy's face.

'He's tramming,' Andy said, snapping shut his book and slinging it over his shoulder into the back. 'Let's give him a pull and see where the fire is, shall we?'

Quickly engaging first gear, Andy stamped on the accelerator and the wheels spun, churning up loose chippings, then, whipping the steering down hard right, he pulled onto the glistening road in the direction of the bolting Escort.

Hunter gripped the sides of his seat, repeatedly switching his gaze from Andy, as he effortlessly slipped through the gears, to the windscreen, where he saw they were making ground on the gold car. They were hitting 75 mph.

Andy flicked on the blue strobe lights and hit full beam.

Ahead, Hunter saw the brake lights on the Ford illuminate. The distance between them was ever narrowing and the Escort Ghia began indicating left.

Andy braked sharply and pulled up behind it, switching on his hazards as he jumped out, shouting back, 'Check it on PNC.'

Hunter snatched up the radio handset and called in the registration number of the car. Less than a minute later the control room operator was giving back details of an owner from the nearby village of Old Denaby. It wasn't recorded as stolen.

Hunter joined Andy — who was just issuing a rollicking to the driver — a man in his 30s, with collar-length dark hair and a face badly scarred by acne, who was being most apologetic — and passed on the information the operator had given him.

Andy said to the driver, 'Take this as a warning. This is a 60 mph road — keep it down in future.'

The man replied, 'Thank you, officer, I will. As I say, I've only just bought the car and the road was so clear that I opened her up. I hadn't realised I was going that fast.' He sighed gratefully and turned the ignition. There was no response. He turned the key again — nothing. He exchanged glances with Andy and then Hunter.

Hunter noted sweat forming on his brow.

He said, 'I think it must be the starter motor jammed.'

Andy looked at Hunter and threw him a nod. 'Come on, we'll give him a push.'

The pair heaved themselves against the back of the Escort and began to push. They had only travelled a few yards when it roared into life and after a few revs the driver shouted, 'Thank you!', and set off steadily in the direction of the A1.

Rubbing his hands, Andy turned to Hunter. 'That's our good deed for the day.'

As they were climbing back into the patrol car, they picked up on the sound of another speeding car heading towards them.

'Bloody hell, it's like Le Man's this afternoon,' Andy said, pulling his leg back out and stepping into the side of the road, just as a rocketing car appeared from the bend 50 yards down the road.

Andy started waving his hands in the air, signalling it to stop.

The bonnet of the Rover dipped, followed by a long screech, as tyres skidded across wet tarmac. It juddered and bucked before grinding to a halt.

Hunter could see there were two men in the car. The driver looked to be late 40s, with greying hair, and the passenger, a lot younger, probably early 20s. Hunter had not even moved when the passenger door shot open and the young man hurriedly leapt out, thrusting out an arm and aiming it in the direction of the gold Escort, which by now, was just a dot in the distance.

He shouted, 'That car, the Escort, it's mine. It's just been nicked.'

Hunter saw Andy's jaw drop. He could feel blood rushing into his own face with embarrassment. Before he had time to say anything, Andy had reacted, throwing open the driver's door and jumping into the car.

'Don't worry, we'll get him,' Andy shouted, gunning the engine and pulling his door shut.

Hunter hadn't even had time to fasten his belt before they were shooting onto the road.

Within seconds, Andy was whipping through the gears, thrashing the engine, soon edging the needle towards 80.

It wasn't long before the dot on the horizon was becoming recognisable as the stolen Ford Escort Ghia they had stopped only minutes earlier.

Andy squeezed more from the patrol car, while Hunter was calling in the chase over the radio. He couldn't hide the excitement in his voice — a buzz was coursing through every vein in his body. He was hyper alert.

Soon the cars were bumper to bumper, then they were alongside, edging their car towards the driver's side of the stolen Escort.

The Ford bobbled as they lined up alongside, and Hunter caught the look of panic in the thief's heavily pockmarked face as he fought with the steering.

A split-second later the Escort snaked and Andy pulled away as it began to lose control. Blue smoke burned from the rear wheels and the Escort began to lurch sideways in a crab-like movement. As it turned 180 degrees, it went into a half spin, and then bounced across the road, smashing into the grass verge. It was only the height of the verge that stopped it rolling over.

Andy slung the panda hard left and slewed to a skidding halt across the front of the Ford, cutting off any escape. Hunter was leaping out of passenger side just as the driver's door of the stolen Escort was starting to open, and he kicked out. There was a sickening crunch followed by an ear-splitting scream. Hunter realised he had caught the thief's leg in the door and he couldn't help but let out a smirk.

Andy was beside Hunter in seconds, yanking open the door and the driver fell into the roadway in a painful heap. Clasping his hands around his shins, he cried, 'Fucking hell, there was no need for that.'

'That serves you right for being a cheeky little bastard,' shouted Andy. 'And you're under arrest for nicking this car.'

Screwing up his face, the thief moaned, 'Well, you two wankers helped me!'

Hunter stood uncomfortably to attention beside Andy Sharp, studying the duty inspector across the desk. There was a mug of coffee resting on a coaster and he could smell the aroma; his senses were still heightened from the adrenalin rush two hours ago. Following the booking in of their car thief at the custody suite, they had done a check on the name the man had given them, and it transpired that Dale Swallow was a well-known villain from Newcastle who specialised in stealing high performance vehicles. He was part of a car ringing team from the North East who was circulated as wanted for numerous offences of burglary.

Yet, in spite of the buzz surging through him, Hunter was also nervous. He wondered if the beaming smile the inspector threw at them was merely a ruse to throw them off-guard, before he tore into them for letting the car thief go in the first place.

The inspector said, 'Well done, you two. Run the job past me again.'

Andy did the talking while Hunter listened.

Slowly, Andy gave a blow by blow account of their encounter with, and then capture of, Dale Swallow, omitting the part about them helping him with a push-start. Hiding a gulp in his throat, Hunter again checked the inspector's face as Andy finished. His smile had grown wider.

'Forces up and down the country have been after this guy for some time,' he said. 'This'll mean a District Commendation for the pair of you. Well done once again.'

As Andy closed the inspector's door behind him, Hunter let out a nervous breath. The high had now gone and he was a quaking mess.

Andy tapped him on the shoulder. 'You heard what the inspector said — commendation. Now, don't spoil it. There's only you and I know what went on out there. Keep it that way.' He threw Hunter a wink. 'Come on, we've got our statements to do.'

CHAPTER EIGHT

Anita Thompson flashed open her eyes. Something had disturbed her, and for a moment she lay in her bed, listening and roaming her eyes around her bedroom, trying to penetrate the gloom. There was a noise at the far end of her bungalow. She thought it sounded like footsteps walking across the tiled kitchen floor.

Is it Julie? Is it time to get up?

She was confused. It was still dark.

Now it sounded as if someone was shuffling around in the hallway.

Lifting her head from the pillow, she leaned across and switched on the bedside light.

'Hello,' she called out. 'Julie, is that you?'

Silence.

Anita pushed aside the sheets and swung her legs out of bed. She grimaced as a sharp pain registered in her right hip. Her arthritis was playing up again. She waited for it to subside and then planted her feet on the floor, tracing out her toes in the carpet, her eyes searching out her slippers.

She took her time sliding them on. Then dragging her dressing gown from off the bottom of her bed she clenched her back muscles to support her and eased herself up.

Putting an arm through one sleeve she listened again. Nothing! She shrugged her shoulders. She must have been mistaken.

Never mind, I'm up now. I'll get myself a drink.

Opening the door into the hallway, she was confronted by a bright beam of light that took her by surprise, making her heart lurch, and it caused her to step back, clutching her chest.

The beam lowered and behind it she could make out the dark silhouette of someone standing by the doorway that connected the kitchen.

'Who are you?' she yelled. 'What are you doing in my house?'

'Police!'

'Police. What's the matter?' Anita answered back. Her heart was thumping against her chest.

'Your back door was unlocked. I'm just checking everything's all right.'

'Show me your identification.'

The dark figure stepped towards her, and it looked as if he was reaching inside his coat, but, as he neared, she caught a glimpse of his head and immediately saw that he was wearing a ski mask. Her heart picked up again, and she knew what she should have done, but her legs wouldn't let her. A panicky fear enveloped her and froze her solid to the floor.

He took a step toward her, and Anita let out the start of a scream, which didn't finish because his fist smacked her in the mouth. The punch rocked her sideways, buffeting her against the wall. She choked back the remainder of her cry as she tried to stop herself falling.

The intruder grabbed the front of her dressing gown, hoisting her towards his menacing face.

'I'll fucking kill you if you scream!'

She noticed that his breath smelt strongly of stale cigarettes. Her husband, John, used to smoke. Three years before he died from complications arising from his COPD, he told her he'd quit, but she still used to smell it on his breath when he had sneaked one in the garage.

'Where's your fucking money? Tell me where it is now, or I'll hurt you,' snarled the burglar.

She wanted to tell him that she didn't have much, only what was in her purse, but the words wouldn't come out. Her chest was getting tighter. The breath caught in her throat.

He began shaking her and shouting.

Anita couldn't make out what he was saying. The sound seemed distant. Bright flashes and stars cascaded before her eyes. She thought she heard her John calling after her and she smiled to herself. Then she realised it couldn't be her John. He'd been dead three years this month.

In the upstairs rest area of Barnwell Station, Roger and Andy were playing pool, and Hunter had just plated up the sausage egg and bacon he had cooked in the small kitchen for his morning breakfast, when the door to the corridor opened and Sergeant Marrison stuck his head through the gap.

'Meal times over I'm afraid, lads,' he announced. 'We've just taken a call from a woman who says she's found her mother unconscious in bed and she doesn't know if she's fallen or if someone's attacked her. Ambulance are on route.' He stepped through and handed Roger a slip of paper. 'That's the address, check it out to make sure it's not a repeat of what's just happened to June Waring.' Turning back to the door, he added, 'I'm just going to let CID know.'

Roger and Andy laid down their cues on the table, picked up their NATO style pullovers and hurriedly slipped them on.

Hunter flicked his eyes between his plated breakfast and colleagues. 'What should I do with this? I've only just cooked it.'

'You've no time to eat it. You'll have to microwave it when you get back,' Roger replied, heading for the door.

As Hunter confined his freshly-cooked breakfast to the microwave, he let out a heavy sigh. He hoped against hope it would still be there when he got back from the job; he had already learned that his colleagues had a habit of helping themselves to food left lying around. Just before he closed the door, he grabbed one of the two sausages and popped it into his mouth.

The ambulance was just pulling up behind them when they arrived at the bungalow in Montagu Close, a small cul-de-sac made up of similar style bungalows. Hunter was first out, closely followed by Andy.

Heading for the front door, Hunter was distracted by a woman's call from the driveway to his left and took a deviation where he saw a dark-haired, mid-40s lady scurrying toward them.

'It's my mum. Hurry, please. I don't know what's happened to her. Her face is a right mess. I can't wake her up,' the woman pleaded.

Hunter saw the distressed look in her face and upped his pace.

'She's this way,' the woman said, turning on her heel to the rear of the house.

Hunter and Andy followed her to the bungalow where she showed them into the kitchen.

'She's in the front bedroom on your left,' she said, pointing ahead and moving to one side to let them pass.

Hunter was first through the doorway into the bedroom. The first thing he noticed was how neat everything was, which surprised him given the nature of the call. The curtains were open and the room was well lit, giving a good view of a double bed with a crimson headboard, which was covered by a flower-pattern duvet. It looked like it had just been made.

Poking above the duvet, resting between two sets of pillows, was an elderly woman's face, eyes shut, that he immediately saw had taken a serious battering. Both eye sockets were dark purple and swollen, as was the bridge of her nose, and her mouth was crusted with blood.

These injuries are not fresh, he told himself, bending closer to see if she was breathing.

'Bloody hell, what a mess,' Andy Sharp exclaimed, looking over Hunter's shoulder.

Hunter had to get really close before he heard her breathing, and couldn't help but notice how shallow and laboured she sounded. Behind him, he was conscious of activity and, lifting up his head, he saw that the paramedics had come in — a man and a woman — and Roger was also there with the daughter who had called them. She had her hands to her mouth and looked to be in a state of shock.

Hunter moved aside to let the paramedics start their work and returned to the doorway.

'Shall we go in the lounge?' Hunter said, trying his best to sound calm.

The lounge was in a state of darkness and Hunter pulled back the curtains. As the light streamed in through the large bay window, he saw that it was neatly furnished, though dated, with a 1970s green and brown patterned carpet, and a green Dralon three-piece suite. The gas fire was surrounded by dressed stone, which stretched into the alcoves. In the right hand alcove sat the TV. Nao figurines sat on the mantelpiece and a couple of seascape prints adorned the wall behind the sofa. Like the bedroom, nothing seemed out of place.

The daughter dropped down into one of the chairs, stating, 'I hope to God she's going to be all right.'

Roger took the other chair and Hunter and Andy sat beside one another on the sofa.

Roger first asked the lady her name and some details about her mother. She told him she was Julie Burton and that her mother was called Anita Thompson. Anita was 64 years old, a widow, and she had lived at this address for almost 15 years.

'Now, tell me how you found her like this,' said Roger, leaning forward and resting his arms on his thighs.

'I don't know how she's got like that,' answered Julie, looking first at Roger and then swinging her gaze towards Hunter and Andy. 'I found her half an hour ago. We go shopping on Thursday's and have lunch out. I came as normal at nine o'clock and was surprised to see all the curtains closed. I thought at first … well, you know, that something bad had happened. Not like this … but that she might have passed away. I let myself in…'

'Was the door locked?' interrupted Roger.

Julie nodded. 'I always use the kitchen door and that was. I haven't checked the front door.'

'What happened when you came in?'

'Well, as I say, I was a little nervous because of the curtains being closed and so first of all I called her. When she didn't answer, I came through to her bedroom and that's when I saw her laid like that, and well, as I say, I thought the worse. I called her again and opened the curtains and that's when I saw her face.' She threw her hands to her mouth. 'Oh my God! Then I phoned for the ambulance.'

'Was she tucked up like she is now?' Hunter asked.

'Yes.'

'Could she have fallen?'

Julie shrugged her shoulders. 'She never has before. She suffers from a little arthritis, but she's good on her legs. She goes out most days.'

'I know this might seem a strange question, Julie, but do you know anyone who would have done this to her? Has she fallen out with anyone that would cause her harm?'

'Mum? No! Mum never has a bad word to say about anyone. She gets on with everyone round here.'

Roger rose from the chair. 'Do you mind if we have a look around, Julie, while the paramedics sort out your mum?'

'Why? Do you think someone might have broken in?'

'We just need to have a look around, to check things out.'

'I'm sure Mum'll not mind.'

'We'll not disturb things.' Roger turned to Hunter and Andy. 'Andy, would you mind getting some more details from Julie? And me and Hunter will have a look around.'

Hunter followed Roger out into the hall, where they popped their heads through the door of the bedroom to see the paramedics working on Anita. They saw that the duvet had been rolled back revealing a petite lady wearing a pink and white nightdress, the front of it unbuttoned. The pair were conducting an examination of her face.

'How is she?' Roger enquired.

The female paramedic turned her head. 'She's not good. We're just doing some final checks and then we need to get her to hospital as soon as possible.'

'What about her injuries? Can you tell if they're from a fall, or if she's been attacked?'

'This definitely looks like she's been attacked,' the woman responded.

'The injuries are just to her face, and they are severe, as you can see,' the man added. 'Bruising like this would suggest her nose is broken and I'm guessing her eye sockets as well. When someone suffers a fall, you tend to find bruising to the knees and hands where they've tried to stop themselves, and there are none.'

'Okay, thank you. As soon as you're good to go, can you let me know, and one of us will travel through with her to the hospital, just in case she says anything?' said Roger.

The paramedics nodded and returned to their patient.

'Come, let's have a look around, and then I'll update the control room. We need CID down here and SOCO.'

Hunter and Roger slowly made their way down the hallway, heading towards the kitchen. A couple of yards from the kitchen Hunter spotted a couple of stains halfway up the wall to his right. He stopped and scrutinised them. The marks were light brown and smudged. As he looked closer, he noticed other marks around the first lot that were less transparent. He sought out Roger's eyes and said, 'Blood?'

Roger took a look. 'I would say it is, but it looks like someone's tried to clean it up.'

They carefully scanned a wider area of the wall and then switched their gaze to the opposite wall, but they couldn't see any further marks and moved into the kitchen. Like the remainder of the house, this was also neat and tidy.

Roger checked the door, without touching the surface, and then made his way to the window by the sink. He had only been looking a couple of seconds when he uttered, 'My, my, my.'

Hunter joined his tutor. 'Found something?'

Roger pointed to a small hole in the wooden casement of the window, a centimetre below the catch. 'I haven't seen anything like this in years.' He crooked his finger at Hunter. 'Follow me.'

Roger took Hunter outside and pointed at the same section of the window where there was another small hole leading through to the one inside.

'Know what this is?' Roger asked.

Hunter threw him a puzzled look. 'At the risk of sounding stupid — a small hole.'

'But do you know what it's been done with?'

'A drill?'

Roger tapped Hunter's shoulder briskly. 'Exactly. We used to call these brace-and-bit burglaries. Many years ago, Burglar Bill would come along with a hand-held brace-and-bit, drill a small hole below the window catch, push a rod through and unhinge the latch, and then climb through and take what he wanted. The good burglars were so quiet, and made so little mess, that the occupants didn't realise they'd been broken into, sometimes for days.' Roger's mouth tightened. 'My guess is that Anita disturbed our burglar and got those injuries as a result. We need to call this in. We've got ourselves an aggravated burglary.'

CHAPTER NINE

CID turned up ten minutes after the ambulance had left. Andy Sharpe had travelled in the back with Anita Thompson, just in case she regained consciousness and mentioned anything about her attacker. The daughter, Julie, had also gone as well. Hunter had taken up guard duty at the top of the drive, while Roger had started canvassing the immediate neighbours, to determine if any of them had seen or heard anything.

It was DC John Vickers who turned up again, and this time his passenger was Barry Newstead. As he watched Barry climb out of the car Hunter experienced a sense of unease. He saw that Barry hadn't changed a bit in the three years since he had last seen him. His dark mop of curly hair was still shapeless and his dark bushy moustache needed a trim. His manner of dress hadn't changed either; his suit was a different colour — dark grey — but it was still the same style and looked as though he'd slept in it. Since the murder of his girlfriend, Hunter had spoken over the phone with Barry regarding the investigation, but his last face to face with him had been as a suspect in a police interview room, and as he watched Barry sauntering towards him a vision of that moment floated into his head, unnerving him further.

'Look who I've dragged along to see you,' John Vickers announced joyfully as he approached. He was holding a clipboard which he held out for Hunter to take. 'You know the drill by now. You make a note of everyone who comes and goes, and the only people allowed in here are myself and Barry and Scenes of Crime, unless I say so.'

'Got that,' said Hunter, taking the clipboard.

'Good man. SOCO are on their way but before they get here I want you to tell me everything you've done and show me where you think our burglar got in.'

As Hunter turned to go back down the drive, Barry said, 'I'd heard you'd got in the job, and John told me he'd seen you in Mexborough Row. How's it going? Enjoying it?'

Hunter gave him a sideways look. 'Really good, thank you. A lot different to what I thought.'

Barry laughed. 'I bet it is. They keep most of this stuff hidden from you at training school. If recruits really knew what they were going to be dealing with most would resign before the course had finished.'

'I think it's better than I thought it would be.'

Barry patted his shoulder. 'That's what I like to hear. But then, not every probationer gets a murder and now this in one week — that's more excitement than I had.'

They got to the bottom of the drive and Hunter took them to the back of the bungalow and showed them the hole drilled into the kitchen window. 'Roger mentioned something about a brace-and-bit burglar doing this.'

Both Barry and John nodded.

'I haven't heard of, or seen, this type of MO in a long time,' Barry said, examining the drilled hole in the wooden casement. 'In fact, the last time I dealt with anything like this was back in the early 80s.'

'No signs of a search inside?' John Vickers questioned.

Hunter shook his head. 'Doesn't look like it. Not a thing's out of place. The daughter was here and she can't see anything missing.'

'And you found the occupant in her bed?' John quizzed.

'Tucked up, unconscious. Her face has taken a real battering.'

'Do we know if that's where she was attacked?'

Hunter shrugged his shoulders. 'We found what we think are bloodstains on the hallway wall. It looks as though someone has tried to clean them up. I can show you if you want?'

'So you think our victim might have been attacked in the hallway and then placed unconscious in her bed? Is that what you're suggesting?' Barry said.

'I don't know, Mr Newstead. I'm just saying what me and Roger have found.'

Barry grinned. 'You don't need to call me Mr Newstead now, young Kerr. You're one of us now and I'm not a gaffer. Just call me Barry.'

Hunter blushed.

'Come on, show me these marks, and show me which bedroom you found her in, and then you can go and keep an eye on things at the front. Once SOCO get here, I want you to help Roger with the house-to-house, okay?'

Hunter was just about to reply when his radio crackled into life. It was Andy Sharpe speaking from the hospital, asking for CID. John Vickers held out his hand and Hunter handed over his radio.

The three of them crowded around the radio as Andy provided an update about Anita Thompson's condition. He explained she was in intensive care, had regained consciousness but was in a great deal of pain, and was confused about what had happened to her, so he hadn't been able to get anything from her about her attack. He said she'd had a scan, which had revealed her right cheekbone was fractured, as was her nose and she had severe swelling to her face. The injuries she had suffered were what they were expecting to hear. What they weren't anticipating was the news he finished his report with. When the radio message ended, Hunter, John and Barry all stared at one another.

John was the first to respond. 'Fuck me, she's been raped. We're dealing with another rape.'

Hunter strolled along the road, checking the last house-to-house questionnaire he and Roger had completed. They had now seen all the occupants on Montagu Close and all of them had been shocked at the news of the attack — Hunter and Roger hadn't revealed that their neighbour had been raped — but none of them had been able to provide anything helpful to assist the investigation.

As they made their way back to Anita Thompson's to liaise with John and Barry, Hunter turned to Roger. 'Do you think it's the same person?'

'I don't know,' Roger answered. 'When you look at them both for comparison, June Waring and Anita Thompson's lifestyles are about as opposite ends of the spectrum as they can get. And with Anita, it definitely looks as though she's been broken into, from the hole drilled into the kitchen window, whereas with June's place, there was no sign of a break-in at all. There are similarities, in that both houses were locked up after the attack, and both of them were raped, but that might just be a coincidence. Anyway, I wouldn't worry about it. We're not going to be involved anymore after today. We'll have to just wait and see till they nick whoever's done both jobs.'

By the time they got back to the bungalow Scenes of Crime we're just finishing their work. John Vickers took the paperwork from them, thanked them, and told them that he and Barry were locking the place up and going through to the hospital to speak with Mrs Thompson and her daughter. 'We're going to get someone from the after's shift to come and guard the place, so you two can go back to the station. If we need anything else, we'll be in touch,' John added.

Roger and Hunter made their way back to the car. Opening the car door, Roger said, 'Listen, Hunter, I've got to go and get a statement for an accident I'm dealing with. I've had to put it off twice and the sergeant's going to be on my back if I don't get the file in soon. If you want to walk back to the station, I'll nip and get it, and see you back at the nick, okay?'

Hunter responded with a quick shrug, and set off walking.

Half an hour into his stroll, Hunter's stomach started churning. He checked his watch — one o'clock — an hour to go and his shift was over. He thought about the breakfast he had cooked that morning that was still in the microwave. He guessed by now someone would have discovered it and it would no longer be there. Despite the numerous cups of tea he'd drunk, and biscuits he'd eaten during the form filling, he was running on empty. He was also busting for a piss.

He looked up and down the street he was on, gathering his bearings. He realised that he was approaching an area at the end of the road which had been earmarked for development — several rows of old Victorian terracing were in the early stages of demolition. It was the ideal place to go, he thought — there would still be toilets in some of the outbuildings.

He picked up his pace and, turning the corner, he spotted the long row of boarded up terracing stretching out before him. Then, tramping across waste ground he soon reached the rear of the old Victorian housing.

He checked half a dozen outhouses before he found one with a toilet that hadn't been vandalised.

Hunter was just fastening up his trousers when a clattering noise, followed by a curse made him jump. Stiffening, he held his breath and listened. Another burst of noise sounded that

Hunter recognised as metal upon metal. He eased open the door and poked out his head.

It was just starting to rain and Hunter hutched up the collar of his gaberdine and stepped out from the outbuilding. Twenty yards away, he spotted a bent-over man edging backwards out of one of the empty houses, dragging something through the doorway. Hunter set off at a pace across the strip of broken concrete that separated them. Ten yards in, the man straightened and Hunter immediately recognised George Arthur Hudson.

Hunter commanded, 'What are you doing, Jud?'

Jud span around, his face displaying a mix of shock, surprise and amazement. He coughed a couple of times before replying, 'Fucking hell, young 'un, you made me jump.'

'What're you up to?'

'That's a nice greeting. I'm not up to owt. Just doing my job, that's all.'

Hunter took a few steps closer. Behind Jud, he saw a wheelbarrow containing a couple of copper hot water cylinders. 'What're you doing with that lot?'

'I've just said, doing my job.'

Hunter studied Jud's face. 'Explain.'

'I'm on the security here. We've had a load of break-ins. Folks nicking the scrap. It's my job to lock it in the compound for the night.' Jud pointed out metal mesh security fencing surrounding several portacabins a hundred yards away. 'It's going in there.'

Scrutinising the contents of the wheelbarrow, Hunter checked his face again. Jud had a blank look. 'Okay, well, make sure you do that.'

Jud bent down and picked up the handles of the wheelbarrow. 'Sure, no problem.' Pushing the laden barrow in the direction of the builder's compound, he called back over his shoulder, 'It's good to see you around here, there's no end of thieves about, you know.'

Watching Jud go, Hunter couldn't help but smile.

CHAPTER TEN

On the garage forecourt, Hunter carried out his second scrutiny of the fire-engine-red F-registered, Ford Fiesta XR2, with black trim and black interior, admiring the pepperpot-style alloy wheels and front grill twin spotlights as standard. This is just what he had been saving up for.

'Well, what do you think?' asked the salesman. 'She's been well looked after, regularly serviced, and only 20,000 on the clock. That's well under mileage for a three-year-old car.'

Hunter eyed his dad for a response.

'Well, it's nice, son, but what do you think about the Volvo over there?'

Hunter followed the line of Jock's pointing finger to the D-reg, dark-blue Volvo 240, parked against the far wall, and looked back at him, horrified. 'Dad! It's an old man's car. And it's two years older than this.'

Jock shrugged his shoulders in a matter-of-fact way. 'It's practical and safe. It's one of the safest cars in Europe.' Then following a brief pause, he said, 'What about a Rover like mine? That's reliable.'

'Dad, this is a young man's car,' Hunter responded, dragging his eyes back to the Fiesta. 'I like it.'

'It is very sporty, and it holds well on the road,' said the salesman.

'I've no doubt it does, but you'll get more for your money with that Volvo,' Jock countered.

'I like it,' Hunter said resolutely.

'Your mum'll have a fit.'

'Mum's not driving it,' Hunter answered.

'True.' Jock shrugged. Then he said, 'It's your money. If you like it, go for it. You only live once.' Slipping his hands in his pocket, he added, 'You know, I'm going to get it in the neck when she sees this wee beastie pull on to the drive.'

Both Hunter and the salesman burst out laughing.

'Shall we go and sort out the paperwork then?' said the salesman.

On the A169, over the North York Moors, as the minivan in front turned off towards Goathland, Hunter got his first stretch of open road since they had passed the Hole of Horcum and put his foot down, edging his XR2 to 70 mph. 'Well, what do you think?' he said, gripping the steering wheel, turning his head slightly and getting a glimpse of Beth's pretty face displaying a schoolgirl grin.

'It's a car,' she answered nonchalantly.

'It's not just a car, it's sex on wheels.'

Beth gave a snort of laughter. 'I don't know, what is it about men and cars?'

Hunter laughed with her, and then seeing the narrow bridge and sharp bend coming up ahead, focussed his eyes back on the road and eased off the accelerator, slowing down and braking. As he turned into the bend, he geared down and began accelerating again for the climb up to Blue Bank where they would get their first view of their Whitby destination.

As he got another glimpse of Beth's smiling face, he felt a sense of excitement run through him. He had been so glad last night when she had accepted his invite for them to go up to Whitby. She'd told him she had never been, which surprised him, and he replied by telling her he would take her for the best fish and chips in Yorkshire.

Half an hour later, they entered Whitby, and Hunter took the road after the railway station where he knew there was a large car park. As they got out of the car they were met by a sharp wind that was a good deal colder than when they had set off, and both of them were now glad they had put in their padded coats.

As they strolled into town, Beth slipped her arm through his and drew him close. They browsed in a couple of shops before Hunter guided her towards the old market place where the narrow, cobbled streets were lined by a variety of quaint shops. As they window-shopped, Hunter couldn't keep his eyes off Beth, whose long blonde hair was now loose and flowing, unlike the first time he'd seen her a fortnight ago, when she had been in uniform and it had been tied up.

As he watched her swipe back wisps of hair from her face, he had to pinch himself that she'd given him her phone number. At the same time, he also felt a deal of guilt because of Polly. He'd not been out with any girl since her murder, and he hoped that those who knew Polly, particularly her parents, wouldn't think he was betraying her memory.

Hunter steered Beth towards the Magpie Cafe, telling her it served up the best fish and chips he'd tasted.

There was only a small queue outside the distinctive black and white building, and inside ten minutes, they were seated at one of the upstairs tables, looking out over the quayside.

Hunter found conversation with Beth easy and he feasted on her sparkly blue eyes as they talked about their homelife and schooling. Neither of them had got any brothers or sisters, and Hunter learned that her father was in the fire service and her mother a primary school teacher.

He told Beth that he had been born in Scotland, that his father had represented Scotland in the Commonwealth games for boxing and been a professional fighter for a short time, but following a bad injury to his forehead from a fight, he'd had to give it up and had bought a gym in Barnwell setting up his own Boxing Academy.

That had led them to talk about their choice of careers. She told him that her favourite aunt had been a nurse and that's all she had ever wanted to do. In return, he opened up about Polly's murder, telling her his first choice had been to go to art school but all that had changed following her death and that was his reason for joining the police.

As he'd finished telling her, Beth reached across and touched his arm. 'Oh, that's awful,' she said, offering him a sympathetic look. 'I remember reading about that and seeing it on the news. That must have been such a shock.'

Hunter told her that her killer still hadn't been caught, and he was hopeful that one day he would be, and that he would be the one who caught him, and then he moved the conversation on quickly, telling her some of the things he been involved in since joining the police, including the domestic incident with Jack and Alice Paynton, which had resulted in their meeting in A & E.

Beth told him some of her nursing anecdotes, including pranks that she and her colleagues had played on one another, and it was then that he told her of the initiation hoax he had suffered at the hands of his team mates, which brought howls of laughter from her, causing diners to turn their heads, embarrassing them both.

They ate their fish and chips hungrily, Beth telling him that they were worth waiting for, and then, jointly paying the bill, they left. Outside, it had started to rain and initially they dipped in and out of shops to avoid it, but after twenty minutes it had grown in strength and they both agreed to cut short their trip, jogging back to the car.

By the time they hit the motorway the wind and rain had grown in strength, buffeting the car, making driving conditions hazardous and both were relieved when two hours later, the sign for South Yorkshire appeared on the roadside.

'Do you fancy a drink?' Hunter asked, pulling off the motorway.

'That would be nice,' Beth answered, her eyes lighting up. 'I was just thinking the same. Those fish and chips have made me dry.'

'I know just the place on a day like this.'

Hunter deviated to Wentworth, a small village preserved in time, where every building was painted Wentworth Green and Cream, their upkeep and status overseen by a charitable trust. There, he pulled into the car park of the Rockingham Arms, an 18th-century pub which had retained all its traditional features.

It was still hammering down, and he and Beth had to dash across the car park to save themselves from a soaking. In the porch, they banged their feet to rid excess water from their shoes and then stepped into the lounge. The moment they entered, they were met by the heat from a blazing log fire in the large grate to their right and it instantly lifted their dampened spirits.

Hunter rubbed his hands, grabbed Beth's attention and pointed out an empty table against one wall that was only a few yards from the fire. 'That looks a good a spot as any,' he said and led the way.

He watched Beth make herself comfortable and asked her what she wanted to drink. She chose lager and Hunter went to the bar. As his cast his eyes around, he saw that the place was relatively quiet with just over half a dozen people in. Four of those were dining.

Setting down the beers, pulling out a chair, and setting his eyes on Beth, he suddenly felt a tightening sensation in his stomach. Her face had a warm orange glow from the fire and he could see the flames reflection dancing in her eyes. In that instant he thought that she looked truly wonderful.

He couldn't resist saying, 'You look lovely.'

'Thank you,' she said, reaching across and squeezing his hand. 'I've had a great day. Pity about the weather at the end but this has made up for it.'

Hunter held on to her hand. He couldn't help but notice how soft it was.

They spent the next few hours in witty conversation, once more touching on their schooling, home life and a bit about work and Hunter couldn't help but think how comfortable he was in Beth's company. More people came into the pub, the majority for food and by 9 pm the place was full. Hunter had switched to coke because he was driving and was beginning to feel bloated. 'Do you fancy some food?' he asked.

'To be honest, I'm not that hungry. And, I've had enough to drink. I'm on days tomorrow and I don't want to end up with a thick head.'

'Want to go home?'

'I don't want to, but I have to. I've got to get my uniform and everything ready for the morning.' She flashed him a smile and her eyes searched out his. 'Do you mind?'

Hunter released a laugh. 'Not at all. I'm on afters tomorrow, so I've got to get my stuff together as well, and I want to go and do a couple of hours at my dad's gym before I start.' Pushing back his chair, he held out his hand for Beth to take and then they made for the door.

Outside, the rain had stopped but a thin veil of misty fog had descended and Hunter hooked an arm around Beth as they sloped back to his car.

He turned on the engine and switched on the car heater and turned to Beth, thanking her for a brilliant day. His gaze fixed hers and he saw her blue eyes glistening. He straightened in his seat and moved towards her, his fingers searching out her hair. He fought to maintain an outward calm as an exciting nervousness crept over him. His hand slid around the back of her slender neck and gently, he pulled her towards him, his mouth opening to her lips.

Then a shadow flashed in the corner of Hunter's eye, and that was followed by a sudden rap on his window, making him jump. He snapped his head sideways to see a beaming face looking in at him.

Harry Hemsworth. One of the last people he would want to meet right now. Harry was the office constable, eking out his time prior to retirement, and was about as brusque and blunt a character as you would wish to meet. Constantly critical of every new aspect of policing and senior officer alike, Hunter spent as little time as he could in his presence.

Harry rapped on the window again and Hunter wound down his window.

'Hey-op, young Kerr. What are we playing at here then?'

'Just on my way home, Harry.'

Harry poked his head through the gap, forcing Hunter back in his seat.

'Let's see who you're tickling tonsils with then.'

'Bog off, Harry. Piss off in the pub.'

'Don't cheek your elders, young 'un, or you'll feel the back of my hand. Now give us a look-see.'

Hunter wanted to sling the car in gear and tear out of the car park but he knew from others at work that Harry was more than capable of carrying out his threat, and to receive a clout from a fellow colleague in this situation would certainly lower his standing, so he leaned to one side.

'Well, if it ain't young Beth Jones,' Harry exclaimed. 'My, you've shot up, haven't you? The last time I saw you, you were knee-high to a grasshopper.' Then, directing his brash voice in Hunter's ear, he said with a grin, 'This'll cost you, Kerr. I'll be having a word with her dad when I see him.' Then grinning even wider, he said with jovial overtones, 'Goodnight. Hope I haven't spoilt your evening,' and headed to the pub.

Hunter was still furious as they pulled up outside Beth's home. He had spent the past 15 minutes apologising for Harry's behaviour, calling him all names under the sun.

'Hunter, you don't need to apologise for him. I know what Harry's like. None of us kids liked him when he was on the beat. We used to run away whenever we saw him. I used to think he was a giant of a man when I was little, now he's just an overweight, old man. He'll probably end up on one of my wards in the next couple of years, then I'll get my own back.'

They both burst out laughing.

Beth leaned across and pecked Hunter's cheek. 'I've had a lovely day. I've really enjoyed your company.'

'Me too. Want to do it again?'

'You bet.'

'Well, I'm on afters for five days now, and then days, and then it's my long weekend off. Shall I give you a ring and we'll fix something up?'

'That'd be great.' Beth leaned in and planted a gentle kiss on Hunter's lips, and then opened the door and trotted towards her house.

Watching her wave back as she let herself in, and then close the front door behind her, Hunter remained for a moment, staring at the closed door, running his hands around the steering wheel of his new car. He had just had his best day, ever.

CHAPTER ELEVEN

In afternoon briefing, cradling a mug of steaming tea, Hunter listened as Sergeant Marrison updated them on the murder of June Waring and the attack on Anita Thompson. He told the group that, for now, both incidents were being treated as separate cases, although there were some similarities. Detectives had now canvassed Mexborough Row and the streets surrounding it, and had tracked down all of June's drinking pals, but, so far, there were no leads. Anita had fully regained consciousness, but was still frail and remained in hospital, and she had provided detectives with a description of her attacker as well as revealing that the man who had raped her had removed her panties and put them in his jean pocket.

'It looks like our offender has taken them away with him,' Sergeant Marrison said, and followed up by providing her description of him as being slim, between 5'8" and 5'10", wearing dark clothing with a ski mask, adding that he was wearing yellow rubber washing-up gloves. 'She's also told detectives that what had stood out about him was his breath. It smelt strongly of stale cigarettes. And there was also an oily smell about him that's making them think that he could be a mechanic of some kind.

'The enquiry team are currently focussing on villains, especially burglars, who work with cars. They've pulled in two with convictions for brace-and-bit burglaries but they had alibis and have been released.'

Sergeant Marrison ended by asking everyone to mention the description they had of Anita Thompson's attacker at every opportunity as they went about their duties. Hunter made a note in his book.

The next piece of information made Hunter's ears prick up.

Marrison read, 'Report of theft of copper boilers two days ago from the houses being knocked down on Cadeby Terrace. The builders say it's the third lot that's been taken in the last ten days.' He looked up from the bulletin and cast his eyes upon the group. 'I want scrap dealer checks done on your travels — see if anyone's weighed them in.'

Hunter didn't hear any more. His heart was pounding so hard, he feared it would burst from his chest. He scoured the faces of his colleagues hoping they had not latched on to his burning face. How could he have been so stupid? What had Roger told him about Jud Hudson?

His mind raced throughout the remainder of the briefing, only half taking in what was being said, as he grappled with what he should do about Jud. As the briefing came to an end, he had the semblance of a plan.

Twenty minutes later, as he steamed towards Jud Hudson's home, Hunter was a smouldering ball of anger, and by the time he reached the three-bedroom council house, he was lathered with sweat.

He rapped loudly.

'Who is it?' a voice shouted from behind the glass door.

Hunter recognised Jud's voice.

'Police, Jud! Open this door before I kick it in!'

Less than ten seconds later, following the sound of bolts being pulled back, Jud flung open the door, cursing beneath his breath, hands pulling a leather belt tight around a pair of camouflage trousers.

'Hey-op, young 'un — is it a social visit? Shall I stick the kettle on?'

Hunter's mind was screaming. He shot out a gloved hand, aiming an index finger at Jud's chest like a pointed gun. 'You can get your coat on — you're under arrest.'

Jud took a step back. 'Whoa! What's up?'

'You know what's up. That gear I caught you barrowing the other night was nicked from the old houses. You told me you were on the security there. I've checked — you've never worked there.'

Jud's face took on a startled look. 'What gear?'

'You know what gear I'm talking about — those copper boilers.'

Jud shook his head. 'Don't know what you're on about. Search the place if you want. You won't find any copper boilers here.'

Hunter darted his finger forward, stabbing Jud in the chest. Jud tried to avoid it and fell backwards against the hall radiator.

Hunter spat out, 'Get your coat on, Jud, we'll sort this out back down the nick.'

'You're gonna look a fool, you know.'

'What?'

Jud returned a sheepish look. 'I don't want to tell you your job or anything, but I ain't gonna cough anything in interview. It's gonna be your word against mine.'

'Your word against mine? I caught you red-handed.'

'And how's that gonna look with your bosses, eh? You let me walk away with stolen gear.'

Hunter was flabbergasted. He couldn't believe Jud's cheek.

'Look, young 'un, give me a break and I'll return the favour.'

Hunter's thoughts were racing. 'What do you mean?'

'You've got your hands full at the moment with June's murder and that attack on that old lass in her bungalow, haven't you?'

'What do you know about those? What do you know about June?'

'I don't know anything at the moment, but I know people. Lots of people. I can ask around for you.'

'You talked about June as if you knew her?'

'I do know her, as such. Not really to talk to, but I do know some of the people she drinks with down at the Stute. I can make some discreet enquiries, can't I? People tell me things that they don't tell you.' After a pause Jud said, 'What's say you and I make each other a deal?'

Hunter fixed him with a penetrating glare.

'Don't look like that at me. We're haggling here over a bit of scrap. You give me a break and I'll get you a promotion.'

Hunter was going to tell him the job didn't work like that but he bit down on his lip. Clearing his throat, he said steadily, 'So I forget what happened the other night, and in return you find out who's attacked the old woman at Montagu Close, and who murdered June? Is that what you're saying?'

Jud pushed himself away from the hall radiator and straightened up. He nodded. 'Exactly.'

Hunter thought about it for a moment. He said, 'You've pissed me off, Jud — no doubt about it. I don't like anyone pulling the wool over my eyes.'

Jud interrupted, 'Look, I know, but like I say, this is just between us. You could take me in and I'll play the system — maybe I get prosecuted or maybe I don't — that's the risk you take. The other way is you let me off for nicking the scrap, and in return, I give you a bell the minute I find out anything. What do you say?'

Hunter pulled back his hand, thinking through what Jud had said. After a few seconds, he replied, 'Let me tell you this, Jud, if this is more of your bullshit, you and I will fall out good style. I'll tell you now, if I don't hear from you within the next fortnight, I'll hound you like there's no tomorrow and I'll put it out all round the estate you're a grass.'

Jud returned a wide-eyed look and nodded eagerly, 'I'll give you a bell — I promise.'

Hunter turned on his heel and left the house without closing the door behind him. Inside he was smarting but he knew Jud Hudson had one up on him. The last thing he wanted was to look the fool in front of his colleagues, especially as this was his probationary period.

CHAPTER TWELVE

In the station report writing room Hunter checked his voicemail. Nothing. It had been five days since his run-in with Jud Hudson and he hadn't heard anything from him. He hoped it wasn't going to be another one of his ruses. He was double-checking his tray to see if anyone had put a note in there from him, when a familiar voice said, 'Your Sergeant's told me to partner up with you today.'

Hunter turned to see PC Grace Kelly standing in the doorway. Grace was the same age as himself and had been on the same intake at training school, and it was she, much to his annoyance at the time, who had pipped him to earn Best Course Student. Grace had also been posted to Barnwell but was currently working with another duty group.

'How come?' Hunter replied, putting away his correspondence tray.

'I should have been at Crown Court today, but a trial has runover, so my case is relisted for tomorrow.'

'Oh yes, your drugs job. Are you feeling nervous?' Hunter asked. Grace had been the talk of their intake because of her undercover role in the capture of a well-known drug dealer supplying to punters in a nightclub in Rotherham. It was highly unusual for any probationer constable to be used in such a delicate operation, but thanks to her excellent use of Patois, courtesy of her father's Jamaican background, she had blended in unsuspected by the dealer, and successfully bought ecstasy from him and arranged the purchase of more. The dealer had been caught in a sting operation with ecstasy to the value of

£50,000 in his possession. He was looking at a lengthy jail term if convicted.

'Bricking it. I haven't even given evidence yet at Magistrates, never mind going to the Crown Court.'

'You'll do all right. It was a good job. I'm jealous.'

'It was scary, I'll tell you. It was exciting at first to be asked, especially by drug squad, but to actually go in that club and do the business with that dealer. I tell you, Hunter, I don't know how I kept it together. Anyway, what are you up to? Done anything exciting yet?'

Hunter told her about finding June Waring's body and about the attack on Anita Thompson.

'Cool.'

'I was disappointed I couldn't be involved in any of the investigation, as such. I'm already thinking about an attachment to CID when I finish my probation. I'd love to be involved in a murder.' After a brief pause, he said, 'Anyway, this is not going to get us any work done, chatting like this. In fact, it'll probably earn us a bollocking from the sergeant. You grab your things and I'll get my gear and we'll go out for a stroll. I haven't got any jobs pending so we can catch up as we're walking.'

The first couple of hours were quiet — there was very little radio traffic — and Hunter and Grace tested each other on the laws they had learned — both were on the same training course in a month's time during which they would have to sit an exam — and Hunter was pleased to learn that his understanding of what he had read was the same as Grace's. After an hour of examining one another's knowledge they both were of the opinion that they would do well in the exam.

On their way back to the station for their meal they decided to put in a dogleg through the industrial estate and give it the once over. Since the clocks had gone back and the nights had got longer there had been a spate of burglaries in the smaller units of late and all officers had been ordered to carry out checks of properties during their patrols. As he and Grace made their security checks, they noted that many of the larger businesses were still in operation, whereas most of the smaller ones had closed for the day and so they focussed their attention on those.

Approaching the final building, a small engineering company that was isolated from the others, they caught sight of a light flashing, lighthouse fashion, through one of the windows and it looked as though it was coming from a torch.

Hunter stopped, pulling up Grace by the arm. The hackles rose at the back of his neck and he exchanged looks with her. He whispered, 'They don't have security on in there, do they?'

Grace shook her head. 'Not that I'm aware of, it's just a small firm.'

'That's what I thought. You radio in, I'm going to check it out.'

As Hunter made his way around the side of the single-storey, flat-roofed building, he could just make out Grace's voice on the radio calling in her suspicions.

Turning the second corner, slipping around to the rear, he spotted a pair of double doors, one of which was slightly ajar, and a cold shiver ran down his spine. Taking the edge off his pace, he tipped up onto the balls of his feet and curled his fingers around his hasp.

Suddenly the door that was partly open exploded outwards, clattering Hunter's chest and knocking him sideways against metal railings. A split-second later a sharp pain registered to the front of his head. He felt his legs melt and he sunk to the ground, a sickening sensation overwhelming him.

As he tried to figure out what had happened, he found himself looking skywards. At the periphery of his vision he caught sight of a shadowy shape hovering above him, and then he felt a series of fast and hard thumps pelting his upper body. It took him a moment to realise he was being repeatedly kicked. In the background he could hear Grace yelling.

He reeled away as another blow caught his face — surprisingly, he felt no pain — and in that same instance an inner strength erupted inside him. Hunter dodged another blow and lashed upwards and out with his foot. He knew he had connected when he heard a crunching sound followed by a loud groan. At the same time, he saw his attacker stumble backwards, his arms windmilling to stop himself falling.

Hunter leapt to his feet and took up a boxing stance. He sprang forward, putting in two quick jabs, a roundhouse to the ribs, followed by an uppercut. Every punch connected.

As his attacker staggered back, Hunter got his first proper look at the assailant and a spark fired in the back of his brain. He was sure he recognised the dark-haired man. Hunter was about to wade in again with more punches when Grace rushed past him, launching herself at the aggressor. She grabbed hold of the man's hair and began tugging.

'Hold him,' Hunter shouted, swinging in a clenched fist. Just before he connected the man yanked back his head and dropped his shoulder. The arc of Hunter's punch flew over the man's head and caught the side of Grace's cheek.

She let out a squeal and released her hold.

Pulling himself free, the man leaned back and swung in a fist.

Hunter saw it coming and ducked. He felt a rush of air brush his cheek as it whipped past his face, missing him completely, but connecting with the right side of Grace's face. The force sent her reeling and she issued another shriek before smacking into the metal railings.

A roar of anger exploded inside Hunter's head and he retaliated with a succession of quick, accurate punches. Within twenty seconds his adversary was in a crumpled heap.

'I've had enough,' the man cried.

Hunter stood above him, staring into his bloodied face. An uncontrollable shake overtook his limbs. He suddenly became conscious of noises around him. He could make out police sirens in the distance coming ever closer. It was a welcoming sound. He grabbed his handcuffs, spun the raider onto his front and clicked the cuffs onto his wrists. Then putting all his weight onto the middle of the man's back he glanced over to Grace. She was sat propped against the railings with her knees pulled towards her. Her right eye was swollen and her lips bloodied.

Using the back of her hand she dabbed at her mouth. She pulled it away and stared at the blood, then she diverted her eyes and met Hunter's gaze. Her serious look quickly gave way to a smile. 'Remind me never to go out with you again. You give a girl far too much excitement in one night.'

When they entered the man's name into the Police National Computer, it became clear that Hunter and Grace's burglar was well known. Mathew David Smith had previous for theft and was currently on bail for burglary after being caught a fortnight ago breaking into the Co-op for cigarettes. Hunter had been right when he had thought he knew him. Mathew's mugshot was pinned up on the briefing room intelligence board. Given this latest offence, he would be going straight to prison on remand.

Hunter presented Smith to the custody sergeant — a seasoned officer who suffered no nonsense — and outlined the circumstances of the arrest. The sergeant glanced at Hunter and Grace and, making note of their injuries — neither of them told the sergeant that Grace's swollen cheek was down to Hunter — responded with, 'Assault on police officers and he's still alive.' Shaking his head, he finished, 'I don't know — this job's going soft.'

Hunter and Grace watched a sorrowful looking Smith being led away to the cells and then they went up to the CID office. The on duty detective was Alec Flynn. When they entered the CID office, he was at his desk, hammering away on a keyboard. He glanced up upon Hunter and Grace's arrival and stopped typing.

Hunter immediately recognised Alec and felt his stomach turnover.

Alec said, 'You two have been busy, haven't you?' He pointed to his personal radio propped up next to the typewriter. 'I was listening in. It's our old friend Matty Smith you've brought in, isn't it?'

Hunter nodded.

Alec settled his gaze upon Hunter. After a few seconds of silence, he said, 'I know you, don't I?'

Hunter nodded again. 'You were involved in my girlfriend's murder. Polly Hayes.'

'That's right. Me and Barry Newstead interviewed you.'

Pursing his bottom lip, Hunter responded with another nod.

Alec let out a short laugh. 'Barry gave you a bit of a grilling, if I recall?'

Hunter did recall. He answered, 'I'll never forget it.'

'Well, you were her boyfriend. And you don't need me to tell you that most murders are committed by those who're close to the victim.' Alec paused, throwing Hunter a thoughtful look. 'Do you know that's the only murder I've been involved in that's not been detected? And I know Barry was gutted when he was told it was being wound up. He's never been defeated before either. We pulled in loads of suspects but never got to the bottom of it.' He kept eye contact with Hunter and shook his head. 'I don't know if you were ever told but we came to the conclusion that the offender wasn't local. One day, he'll be caught. Mark my words.' Withdrawing his gaze, he said, 'Anyway, enough of the reminiscing, let's talk about what you've come to see me about.' Steepling his fingers, he said slowly, 'Mathew David Smith. I've locked up and dealt with Matty quite a few times in the past and he's always come quiet as a mouse. I'm surprised that he's had a go like he has.'

'I think he was desperate,' replied Hunter.

'What do you mean?'

'He told us in the car that he'd done the burglary because he owes money to someone for some smack he had last week. Apparently, the guy came around to his flat this morning and threatened that if he didn't cough up the money by tomorrow, he was going to get his legs broke.'

'Has he said who his dealer is?'

Hunter shook his head. 'We haven't interviewed him properly yet, though he has said that he'll do a deal if we give him bail.'

'Didn't I hear that he's already on bail?'

Hunter nodded. 'For the Co-op burglary a fortnight ago.'

'He's going nowhere then. I'll have to give him some bullshit for his dealer's name. You can leave this with me if you want. I'll get hold of one of the murder team as well. Given his form for burglary, I think they'll want to talk to him about the attack on Anita Thompson.'

Hunter and Grace exchanged glances and both nodded in agreement.

Responding with a brief smile, Alec said, 'Okay then. You two do me your statements and then I'll do the interview and remand file. I'll leave the DI a note for tomorrow morning. I've been in this job 27 years and I've never caught a burglar on the job. You'll both probably get a commendation for this. Well done. Good arrest.'

Hunter beamed as he left the office.

CHAPTER THIRTEEN

In the upstairs rest area, Hunter and Grace were sat opposite one another, biting into their sandwich's, when Sergeant Marrison burst through the doors.

'What are you two doing?' he asked, an urgent edge in his voice.

'We're just having our meal and then we'll be doing our statements for Mathew Smith,' Hunter replied.

'Well, I'm going to have to ask you to turn out before you do that. We've just taken a three-nines from a man who's come across an unconscious woman on the Craggs. All we've got is that she's bleeding from the head, so we don't know if it's a collapse, or if she's been attacked. Ambulance is on its way, and everyone else is tied up, so can you have a look-see at what it is?' The sergeant dropped a set of car keys on the table. 'You can take my car.'

Barnwell Craggs was an isolated area of rock and scrubland one square mile in size, bordering the Tree Estate, and was popular with dog walkers because a path meandering through it led to an area of woodland of roughly the same size. It was here that Polly had been attacked and murdered three years earlier and as Hunter sped to the location it was the only thing on his mind.

As he pulled onto an area of rough ground below the Craggs, he put the headlights on full beam and swept the area. The first thing he saw was an ambulance to the far right but there was no one with it. He knew from previous visits this was where the path up to the top of the Craggs started, and he pulled next to it, braking sharply and cutting the engine.

Grabbing his powerful torch from the backseat, Hunter jumped out, followed by Grace. Before switching on his torch, he scoured the area for presence. 200 metres up the steep incline, he caught sight of two other torches in use, their beams moving around in haphazard fashion, but he was too far away to see who they belonged to.

'Come on,' he said, flicking his head, 'let's see what we've got.'

Hunter set off at a trot, his torch beam sweeping the way ahead, Grace right on his heels. The path was steeper than Hunter anticipated and within 100 metres he was clawing for breath, his chest tight. He could hear Grace suffering the same predicament. By the time he reached the spot where he had seen torchlight his calves were as tight as drums and burning.

He took a deep breath as he approached a group of three people, two of whom were bent over a collapsed form, their torches lighting up a thin pair of legs clad in tights that had several torn holes in them. One foot had on a black heeled shoe, the other was bare, the big toe poking through the torn tights. Hunter could just make out the hem of a checked skirt but couldn't see who it belonged to.

The two people — a man and a woman — bent over the prostrate form were the paramedics and the third person, standing next to them, was a clean-shaven, leonine-headed man in his early 50s, wearing a fawn-coloured coat. Hunter could see he looked concerned.

'What have you got?' Hunter asked, bending down to get a look at.

One of the crew, a faired-haired man in his late 30s, moved to give Hunter a view of their patient. Glancing up, he said,

'This gent here —' dipping his head towards the man in the fawn coat — 'says he found this lady like this 20 minutes ago. She was semi-conscious then and she's beginning to come around a bit since we've been here.' The paramedic shone his torch over the torso of a sprawled and dishevelled woman, who had a bloodied head and face.

Hunter studied her for a moment. She was very slim and petite, clothed in a black coat that was open, revealing a white blouse ripped at the front, exposing a white bra. He thought she looked to be late 50s and he could see that her hair was bleached white-blonde, despite it being heavily matted with blood.

'She was like this when I found her,' the male witness exclaimed nervously. 'I've just come from my mother's. I was on my way home. I thought she was dead.'

'Was it you who made the emergency call, sir?' Grace asked.

The man nodded. 'I had to run back to my mother's and use her phone. Then I came straight back here to wait for the ambulance. Is she going to be all right?'

'So, you don't know if she's collapsed or been attacked? You didn't see anyone?'

'I did hear her scream, but I was right up there.' He pointed up to a gap 50 metres up the rise, beyond the rocks.

Hunter knew that way led to an estate. 'But you didn't see anyone?'

The man shook his head. 'No one. I was a bit nervous about coming down this way when I heard her scream. I waited up there for good few minutes, but I didn't hear anything else and so I came down. I almost tripped over her.'

'She was laid exactly like this? You haven't moved her?'

'No. As I say, I thought she was dead. I bent down and tried talking to her, and I could just make out the blood on her face, and she wasn't moving, so I ran back to my mother's and called for the ambulance and then came straight back here.' After a brief pause, he added, 'I didn't see or hear anyone at all.'

Hunter dropped to one knee beside the paramedics. 'What's her injuries?'

The male paramedic responded, 'She's got a really nasty head wound to the left-hand side and it looks like her nose is broken.' He flashed his torch over her face. Blood covered her philtrum and had trickled into her mouth. Her hair and left side of her face was caked in blood, some dried and some in the stages of congealing. Parts of it were thick. 'I'm not happy about the wound to her head. It looks pretty nasty. Her skull could be fractured. We need to get her to hospital.'

Suddenly the prone woman coughed, splattering droplets of blood. She moaned and blinked open her eyes.

'Can I ask her a quick question?' Hunter asked.

'You can try. She's responding but I don't know how conscious she is. We need to get her to hospital though, sharpish.'

Hunter leaned into the woman and said, 'What's happened to you?'

The woman gazed up at him, her eyelids flickering over extremely dark pupils. She seemed to be having difficulty focussing. 'He tried to rape me,' she rasped.

'Who did?'

'A man! I don't know. He was wearing a mask.' Her words were slow and slurred.

'What kind of mask?'

The lady's eyes started flickering again. This time more rapid. 'Black one, with just his eyes showing. And he was wearing marigolds.'

That last part of the attacker's description pricked Hunter's thoughts. He remembered Anita Thompson describing her attacker as wearing yellow washing-up gloves.

'What's your name, love?' Grace asked softly.

'Elizabeth. Elizabeth Barnett.' She let out a long moan.

'We need to get her to hospital and get her assessed,' said the female paramedic. 'Can you help us with the stretcher?'

'Sure.' Hunter nodded. Pushing himself up, he turned to Grace. 'You get this gent's details, and I'll help get this lady in the ambulance.'

It was a good 20 minutes of careful handling before they got the woman into the ambulance. During that time, the crew had become more concerned about her condition; she had stopped moaning and lapsed back into unconsciousness. After informing the paramedics that someone would be coming to the hospital within the hour to check on her, Hunter watched them go, the ambulance lights flashing and sirens blaring. Then he made his way back up the Craggs, returning to Grace. The witness who had found the woman was no longer there and Grace explained she had taken all his details, done a computer check of him and allowed him to go.

'We need to secure the scene,' Hunter said, sweeping his torch around the flattened area where the woman had been laid.

'I've already tried to see if she left anything, or if there's any evidence of what she was attacked with.' Grace set her torch beam over a palm-sized lump of rock. 'I found this. It's got blood on it. He could have hit her with it.'

Hunter studied the sharp-edged stone lying in the grass and nodded. 'We'll see if we can get someone to join us and help seal this area off and then we'll go back and let CID know what we've got.'

Andy Sharpe joined Hunter and Grace at the scene, helped them secure the area with tape, which they wedged and wound around rocks, and then took up guard while Hunter and Grace returned to the station. On route, Grace did a voters check and found an Elizabeth Barnett living at an address just half a mile from the Craggs. They called at the house but it was in darkness.

Back at the station, before seeking out CID, Grace also put in a call to the hospital, who informed her that Elizabeth had received a fracture to her skull, suffered a bleed to the brain and been taken into surgery. Grace asked if the nurse could put Elizabeth's clothes to one side for evidence, telling her that someone would be there within the next hour.

The lights in the CID office were on but there was no one in.

'I bet Alec's having his meal,' Hunter said, and led the way along the corridor to the kitchen and rest area, where they found Alec Flynn with another detective in the television room. Hunter had seen the other detective about the station — he had been brought in for the murder enquiry — but he didn't know him.

'Now then, I hear you've been dealing with Betty Barnett,' said the detective.

'We've been to the Craggs where a woman's been attacked. She told us her name was Elizabeth Barnett. We think she lives at Denaby Avenue but we haven't been able to confirm that yet,' Grace answered.

'Aye, that's Betty,' said the detective.

'Do you know her?' Grace asked.

'There's not many men who don't know Betty.' He released a gruff chortle, still remaining seated sloppily in the chair. 'She's had more prick than a pincushion.'

Hunter already found himself disliking this man's curt manner and remembered the words of his tutor, Roger, about how some detective's treated others as if they were beneath them.

'She's in a bad way. She's got a fractured skull and she's currently in surgery. At the scene she told us someone had tried to rape her, and the nurse at the hospital has told us she didn't have any underwear on when they undressed her,' continued Grace.

'Pher!' The words blew out through the side of the detective's mouth.

'What's that supposed to mean?' Grace said.

Hunter caught Grace's tetchy tone and suddenly had a bad feeling about where this conversation was going.

'Let's face it, darling, they don't call her Bareback Betty for nothing. She gives it away. She probably went out wearing no knickers.' He released a bluff laugh.

'So, because of her reputation, you're saying she can't have been attacked for the purpose of being raped?' Grace's voice now had an edge of anger.

'I'm saying she's probably making a complaint because he couldn't get it up, she's that ugly.'

'Do you know the reason women don't complain of rape is because of morons like you?'

The detective pushed himself up in his chair. 'The reason most women complain is because they're afraid their husband will find out.'

'Jesus, you really are a fucking moron.'

The overweight detective leaned forward. 'Who on earth do you think you're talking to, young lady? You need putting in your place. You're nothing but a woodentop and a probationer at that. Now, if I was you, I'd run along while I talk to your colleague about this matter.'

Grace took another step forward and Hunter grabbed her by the wrist. 'Come on, Grace, he's not worth it.'

'Probably wrong time of the month, eh?' The beefy detective winked towards Alec Flynn, looking for encouragement.

Hunter saw that Alec looked embarrassed.

Grace shook herself free from Hunter's grasp, took two steps forward, picked up a mug half filled with tea from the coffee table and threw the contents straight at the detective.

Instinctively, trying to avoid the warm tea, he launched himself back, up-tipping the chair, sending him sprawling backwards to the floor, which he hit with a resounding thump, the air exploding from his chest.

There was another half full mug on the table and Grace picked it up and emptied that all over his face and chest as he tried to roll himself up.

The detective let out a startled cry.

'That's for being a knobhead,' Grace heralded loudly and marched out of the room.

In the snug of the George and Dragon pub, Hunter sat across the table from Grace with a pint of beer. She had a glass of white wine. Both wore wide grins.

'Christ, Grace, Keith Saker's face was a picture. I can't believe you did that,' said Hunter.

They had discovered the brusque detective's name from Alec, who had apologised for his colleague's behaviour as he took their report of the attack upon Elizabeth Barnett, promising he would be taking charge of the complaint and would be visiting the hospital before he went off duty.

'What did the inspector say to you?'

'Originally he said I could be in trouble, but as soon as I said I wanted to make a complaint of sexual harassment, he bottled it and said to leave it with him. In other words, he's going to cover it up. Typical.'

'Are you going to take it further?'

'Nah. He's got his just deserts. He'll think twice about saying stuff like that again.' She took a glug of her wine. 'Anyway, I've got more important things to think about. Crown Court tomorrow.'

'It's just a shame we can't be involved in following up Elizabeth's attack. It sounds to me as though it could be the same guy who attacked Anita Thompson. I know Elizabeth didn't manage to say what type of mask her attacker was wearing, but it's too much of a coincidence that two women are attacked by a man wearing a mask and marigold gloves within the space of a week. Also Anita Thompson said that her attacker took off her underwear and put them in his jean pocket before he raped her. That might be the same with Elizabeth. '

CHAPTER FOURTEEN

The next day, Hunter was on morning shift — 6 am to 2 pm — and he had just enough time to grab a cup of tea before being whisked out, back to the Craggs, where he had to relieve the night duty officer and take up guard at the site of Elizabeth Barnett's attack. Temperatures had dipped overnight, leaving behind a hoar frost, and although he was kept relatively busy, heading off dog walkers to divert them away from the crime scene, by 8 am he was frozen to the core, repeatedly stamping his feet to try and invigorate some warmth back into them.

He had learned that Elizabeth had suffered a compound fracture to the skull and she had deteriorated following surgery and was currently in intensive care in an induced coma. DC Alec Flynn had been out to the hospital but because she wasn't conscious there were no new leads as to who had attacked her other than the brief description he and Grace had obtained the night before. Hunter was now waiting for Scenes of Crime to turn up and carry out a forensic examination of the locale, which would hopefully change all that.

Below him, Hunter spotted one of the CID cars pulling onto the rough ground that he had entered by last night and he watched it circle and then park up beside the footpath. The driver's door opened and he saw Barry Newstead hoisting himself out of the car, using the door as support. Barry pulled out his sheepskin coat, slipped it on and then started the steep climb.

As Barry approached, Hunter could hear him wheezing loudly and smiled to himself.

Barry was blowing in his hands as he neared. 'Bloody hell, Hunter, it's parky this morning.'

'How do you think I feel? I've been here two hours already.'

'If it's any consolation I've been in your place at one time or another.' Barry slipped his hands into his pockets. 'SOCO not been yet?"

Hunter shook his head.

'Shouldn't be too long, and, once they've done here, you can take away all the tape and your job's done.'

'Can't come fast enough. I'm freezing, and starving.'

Barry let out a quick laugh. 'Alec tells me you and Grace Kelly had a run in with our Dick Dastardly Detective, Keith Saker?'

Hunter felt himself going red.

Barry placed a hand on Hunter's shoulder. 'Don't feel embarrassed by it. Between you and me, there's a lot of people think what happened to him has been well overdue. He hasn't got any support whatsoever. In fact, Grace is the blue-eyed babe at the moment, after catching that dealer. You tell her from me, when you next see her, that there's a lot of people praising her for standing up to Keith. Tell her, good on her.'

Hunter was pleased to hear that. He would ring Grace once he got back to the station and relay Barry's comments. For a moment he studied Barry who was running his eyes around the scene. When his gaze returned, Hunter said, 'Can I ask you something, Barry?'

Barry gave him a weak smile. 'I think I know what you're going to ask. Polly?'

Hunter nodded.

'I was thinking about her case whilst driving here and I would bet my reputation as a detective that this and Anita Thompson's case are not connected, despite Polly's being found just a stone's throw from here. Polly was not interfered with at all. And she was not beaten, just viciously stabbed. Polly was murdered by a psycho killer and not a rapist. When we have half an hour, you and I will sit down and have a chat about her case, just in case you come across anything similar. Okay?'

'That'd be good, Barry. Thank you.'

It was 11 am before Hunter was released from the scene, and he made his way back to the station, where, the moment he stepped through the door, he was greeted by the inspector who informed him that he and Grace had been put forward for a divisional commander's commendation for the arrest of Mathew David Smith.

Hunter was told that during interview, whilst Mathew had denied any involvement in the attack upon Anita Thompson, he had admitted to committing six other house burglaries and a dozen shoplifting offences and was now on remand in Armley Prison.

Hunter thanked the inspector and, with a spring in his step, skipped upstairs to the rest room to make himself a cuppa before putting in a phone call to inform Grace of the praise they had been given. He knew she was worried about giving evidence and also guessed she might be a little down following her altercation with DC Keith Saker, so this news would be welcoming.

He had just filled the kettle and put aside a cup to make a brew when his radio crackled into life. The control room were informing everyone that a 999 call had just been received from a woman who was being attacked by a man at an address just a few streets from the police station, and knowing it would only take him a couple of minutes to get there if he put in a run,

Hunter dashed from the rest room and bolted back down the stairwell informing the police operator that he was attending.

Dearne View consisted of three blocks of two-storey, flat-roofed, council tenements. Number 18, where the call had come from, was on the first floor of the middle block.

Yanking open the entranceway doors, Hunter bounded up the concrete stairwell to the first floor, where he skidded to a halt trying to steady his heaving chest. He saw that the door to number 18 was open, though the place was eerily quiet. Taking another deep breath, he took a firm grip of his baton, called out 'Police!' and stepped into a gloomy narrow hallway.

Two steps in, he stopped and listened. He caught the muffled sounds of something being dragged behind a partly open door at the far end of the hall and he made towards it. At the door, he stopped, removed his baton, and, using it to push the door open fully, he edged into a lounge filled with warm sunlight that caused him to screw up his eyes. Because of the brightness, he could just make out a blurred shape of someone bending over in the middle of the room and his heart leapt.

But then his focus adjusted and he saw that the silhouette was a slim, ginger-haired woman, who was righting a toppled armchair. She turned to face him as he stepped into the room.

Her face was flushed and Hunter saw that the front of her t-shirt was torn. Two trails of mascara stained her cheeks where she had been crying.

There was no one else around.

'You've made a three-nines call? Someone attacking you?' Hunter pointed to her torn t-shirt. 'What's happened?'

'He's nearly killed me this time.' She rubbed a thumb across her cheek, smudging her mascara further. Then she took a step forward and tilted her head exposing her neck. She pointed to red marks each side of her throat. 'I want him done for this. He tried to strangle me.'

'Who?' said Hunter. 'Is he still here?'

She shook her head. 'No. I managed to get to the phone to you lot. He did a runner just before you got here. He'll probably be heading for his mates or his mum's.' She picked up a discarded cushion from the floor, patted it and dropped it into the armchair she had put back onto its four legs. Then she flopped into the chair. 'I've had enough of him. He'll kill me before long.'

Throughout the short conversation, Hunter had one ear to his radio and he could still make out that officers were speeding towards his location. He held up a finger to shush her and interrupted the radio chatter. 'You can cancel any further assistance. I'm with the complainant now. The offender has left the premises and I'm just getting details,' he said over the airwaves and returned his look to the woman. 'Now, tell me what's happened.'

In between sobs, Hunter learned that she was 23-year-old Kim Davies, and that the man who had attempted to strangle her was her boyfriend of 18 months, Dylan Wolfe, two years her senior. She also told him that this attack wasn't the first time. 'You ask my friends, they'll tell you what he's like towards me. He's threatened me, even when they've been there.'

The name Dylan Wolfe didn't mean anything to Hunter. He asked, 'Have you made a previous complaint? Has he been arrested before?'

Shaking her head, she dragged away her eyes and shied them to her feet. She crossed her ankles. 'I want to report it this time. I've had enough. You ought to have seen the look in his eyes. I'm telling you if I hadn't managed to get to the phone when I did, you'd be dealing with a murder now. His temper's getting worse. It's all that cannabis he's smoking.'

Hunter took out his pocket book. 'I'll just get a few details, and some background and then I'll take a statement.'

'I want to press charges. I want him locked up.'

'If you give a statement, I'll arrest him.'

'Will he be kept locked up? I don't want him coming back here. He really will kill me, you know, especially if he knows I've made a statement against him.'

Hunter shrugged his shoulders. 'Kim, I can lock him up and charge him, but I honestly don't know if he'll be kept there. That will be up to the magistrates. Has he been in trouble for this type of thing before?'

'He's not been reported to the police. But he's done this before to another girl he went out with before me. A friend told me that he'd turned up at the hairdressers where she worked and threatened her. Fortunately, she had two brothers and he got a kicking for it. But the friend who told me this said he threatened to stab the girl. I tell you, I'm really scared.'

'If you give me the addresses of his mum or his mates, I can get him locked up today, but as I say, as for keeping him, that's not up to me.'

'I don't want him coming back here. I've had enough of him.'

'I can arrange that by bailing him to his mum's and tell him he's not to come back here.'

'But that won't stop him.'

'If he comes back here once he's on bail, then we can lock him and he would be put before court for remand.'

'But he could kill me before that.'

Hunter could see that Kim was scared, but he also knew that his hands were tied by the law as to what he could do about her boyfriend coming around to her home once he had been dealt with at the police station. He said, 'Look, give me the addresses of where he is likely to be, and I'll go and lock him up and we can take it from there.'

Kim bit down on her bottom lip. 'I don't want any more hassle from him. If you can't lock him up and keep him, there's no point in me making a complaint.'

'There's every point, Kim. Putting him on bail gives us extra powers to lock him up again and get him on remand.'

'I don't know. I just want him to stop.'

Hunter could tell that Kim was now backtracking on her resolve to have her boyfriend arrested for assaulting her. He said, 'At least if you make a complaint, he'll know he can't get away with this. When he goes to court, it will be a conviction, and it will make it easier for us the next time he does something like this.'

She let out a blast of air and her shoulders dropped. 'I thought you'd just be able to lock him up and that would be it. I don't know now. I think I'm going to ring his mum first. I get on with her. She knows what he's like. He listens to her.'

'Do you want me to have a word with her?'

Kim shook her head. 'No, it'll just make it worse. I'll ring her first.'

'Look, Kim, I can't force you to give a statement but I do think you should think about it. It might make him sit up and think that he can't get away with his behaviour.'

She nodded. 'I'll think about it.'

Hunter let out an exasperated sigh. 'Okay, but let me leave you my name and number, and if you change your mind, you can give me a call.'

She returned a quick nod.

Hunter scribbled his details onto a sheet torn from his information booklet and handed it to Kim. Then he checked she was okay and left. As he closed the door, he felt a great deal of irritation about being powerless to act. In the three months since leaving training school, he had heard his colleagues talk about similar scenarios where wives and girlfriends had refused to make complaints after their partners had battered them, some repeatedly. Even more frustrating, had been the times when many had made formal complaints and then withdrawn them. This was now his second domestic experience and he shared his teammates' exasperations.

CHAPTER FIFTEEN

The next day, following morning briefing, Hunter checked out Dylan Wolfe on the Police National Computer and put in a phone call to the Divisional Collator to see if they had any intelligence about him. There was nothing recorded on any of the police systems, which was disappointing. Hunter made a mental note to telephone Kim Davies later that morning and see if she had changed her mind about making a formal complaint against Dylan.

In the meantime, he had a fair bit of paperwork to complete before the end of his shift; it was his last tour of duty before his long weekend and then it was the start of his night duty when it was always difficult to follow up on enquiries. He was looking forward to the weekend; he had planned to see Beth again, and it was Andy Sharpe's leaving bash on Saturday evening — he had secured his transfer to Road Traffic, a posting he had fought for during the past 18 months and Hunter had been the first person he had shared his good news with.

It took Hunter the best part of an hour to write up his pocket book. He not only had yesterday's domestic report to complete but also the actions he and Grace had taken following the attack upon 58-year-old, Elizabeth Barnett. Elizabeth was still in intensive care in an induced coma with severe swelling to the brain and the only lead, so far, that detectives had to go on was the brief description Elizabeth had given himself and Grace.

Hunter had just put aside his completed pocket book and booted up the word processor to type up his witness statement for the Elizabeth Barnett enquiry when the phone rang, quickly followed by a shout along the corridor from Sergeant Marrison, who told him the call was for him.

Hunter picked it up. 'PC Kerr, can I help you?' He was hoping it was Kim Davies to tell him she wanted to make a complaint.

'PC Kerr, it's me, Jud.'

This was a surprise. He had given up on getting anything from George Hudson. 'What can I do for you, Jud?'

'I said I'd give you a bell if I had anything, didn't I? Well, I've kept my promise.' After a short pause, he continued, 'I'm ringing about Betty. Terrible business that. How is she? Is she all right?'

Hunter straightened in his seat. 'She's in a bad way, Jud. She's in intensive care. Do you know something about the attack on her?'

'Not exactly, young 'un, but I've got a name of someone you can check out. I was in the Stute the other night when Betty was in and I saw who was talking to her. He followed her out of the club just after she left. I know Betty's a bit of a warm 'un, and got a mouth on her, but that was well out of order what he did to her.'

'Who are you talking about, Jud?'

'This is not come from me, if anyone asks, okay. I'm sure it'll be easy to check out what I've just said. There were others in the Stute who'll be able to tell you who Betty was talking to, even if they didn't see him following her out.'

'Who is this person, Jud?'

'Someone I just know as Wolfy. He's in his mid 20s. Bit of a loud-mouth and thinks he's the big "I am" but I don't think he's been done for nought. Smokes that wacky-baccy stuff.'

'Wolfy? No other names, Jud? Do you know where he lives?'

'Sorry, young 'un, I only know him as Wolfy. He lives somewhere on the Tree Estate with his mum, I think. She's called Wendy. She's a regular in the Stute. You just need to ring the club, they'll probably be able to tell you his name. It'll look suspicious if I start asking. I don't want this to come back to me.'

'Okay, Jud, thank you for this. I'll give the club a ring.'

Jud was quiet for a moment, then he said, 'If this comes to ought, that's me and you straight, all right. I've kept my end of the bargain.' On that note, he hung up.

Hunter held on to the handset for a good ten seconds. He could feel his heart fluttering. Was this a breakthrough? He hoped so.

Grabbing the telephone directory, he found the telephone number for Barnwell Working Men's Club and Institute — the proper name of the Stute — and dialled the number. It rang out for the best part of twenty seconds before being answered. It was a woman's voice. 'Hello, Stute,' she said.

'Is that the stewardess?' Hunter asked.

'No, I'm the cleaner. Do you want Joe, the steward? He's down the cellar changing the barrels.'

'Yes, can you get him, please? Will you tell him it's the police?'

Hunter heard the phone being put down, followed by the woman shouting, 'Joe, the police are on the phone wanting to talk to you.'

It was another 30 seconds before Hunter heard the sound of footsteps becoming louder followed by the phone being picked up.

'Hello, can I help you?' The man's voice was slightly out of breath.

'Is that the steward?' Hunter asked.

'Yes, it is. Can I help you?'

'This is PC Kerr, Joe. I'm making an enquiry about one of your members. All I've got is the name Wolfy. He's someone who's in his early 20s.'

That's Dylan you're on about. Dylan Wolfe. Why, what's he been up to?'

Hunter's heart picked up a beat. He answered quickly, 'I'm not sure he's done anything wrong at the moment, I'm just checking up on a nickname I've been given regarding a complaint someone's made. It might not be the same person.'

'Well, he's the only one I know as Wolfy. He's not in here every night. He tends to stick to the weekends. He comes in with his girlfriend and his mum.'

'Thank you, Joe, you've been very helpful.'

'You're welcome.'

As the steward hung up and Hunter listened to the burring sound down the line, he could feel his heart bouncing against his chest.

Hunter did a voters check and found a Wendy and Dylan Wolfe living at 44 Sycamore Crescent, Barnwell. *There can't be two Dylan Wolfe's*, he thought to himself, as he put away the Electoral Role. He could hear the blood pounding between his ears; the adrenalin rush had started. This has to be the same guy who assaulted Kim Davies. Picking up the piece of paper with his scribbled notes, he took the stairs two at a time up to the CID Office. He poked his head through the door but there was no one in, and so he set off down the corridor to the Stolen Vehicle Squads office, which had been commandeered for the Elizabeth Barnett and Anita Thompson enquiry. Barry Newstead was in there, together with John Vickers. Hunter asked Barry if he could speak with him and they stepped out into the corridor.

Hunter took a deep breath, to steady himself before he spoke. 'I've just taken a call from someone who owes me a favour, Barry.' Then he relayed his conversation with Jud, without mentioning George Hudson by name, and followed up with the information from his phone call enquiry with the Steward of the Working Men's Club. He also told him about yesterday's call to Dearne View and the domestic incident involving Kim Davies.

When Hunter finished, Barry said, 'Have you done anything with this information yet?'

Hunter shook his head. 'I've come straight up to tell you, Barry.'

'Good man. It sounds to me as if you might have something here. Have you got anything pressing?'

Hunter told him he hadn't.

'Right, get your things together and I'll meet you downstairs in ten minutes. You and I are going to have a word with this Kim Davies and see what she can tell us about her boyfriend.'

They drove the short distance to Kim Davies's flat. She answered the door on the second knock, dressed in a tight v-neck jumper with jeans, and her ginger hair was tied up revealing a carefully made-up face. She looked a lot different from the previous day, Hunter thought to himself, as he looked her over. In fact, he couldn't help but think how attractive she was and that she deserved someone better. It made him even more angry about Dylan Wolfe assaulting her.

'Oh, it's you,' she said. 'Are you here for Dylan? He's not here. He's at his mum's. And I don't want to make a complaint about him. We've patched things up.'

'We've not come about your domestic,' Barry answered. 'Can we come in a minute?'

She eyed them suspiciously for a few seconds and then stepped aside, opening the door wider. 'There's no lasting damage. He hasn't bruised me. We've sorted things out, honestly. I spoke with him last night and he's sorry.'

'We just want a quick chat with you, Kim,' Barry said, walking in and heading towards the lounge.

Hunter followed and Kim closed the door behind them.

'What do you want to ask me about?' Kim asked. 'Things really are okay between Dylan and me, if that's what you've come for.'

'It's not about that,' said Barry. 'I just want to ask you a couple of questions about where Dylan was the night before last.'

Kim's face screwed into a puzzled look. 'Two nights ago?' she murmured. After a couple of seconds of thinking, she replied, 'He went out for a drink and came back here. Why?'

'Do you know where he went for a drink?' Barry asked.

Her mouth tightened. 'The Stute, I believe. That's what he said.'

'And what time did he get home?'

'About midnight, why?'

'Did you see him when he came home?'

'I'd gone to bed but he woke me up.'

'So did you see him?'

'Can I ask what this is about?'

'It's something we're following up. Would you answer the question, Kim?'

She shrugged her shoulders. 'Yes, I did see him. He woke me up and I came down.'

'What was he like?'

Kim gave them both an intense look. She put the cigarette back in her mouth and took a long inhale, this time releasing the smoke from her nose.

Hunter saw that her hand was shaking.

'What do you mean, what was he like?'

'How did he appear?' asked Barry.

She started to go red. 'He's done something, hasn't he?'

'Why do you say that, Kim?'

'That's why we rowed yesterday. When I came down, he was just in his boxers. He was putting his clothes in the washing machine. I asked him what he was up to and he said he'd fallen down and got his jeans muddy. But I didn't believe him. I thought he'd been seeing someone, and I accused him and we had an argument. I had a go at him yesterday. That's why he attacked me.' She started wringing her hands. 'He's done something, hasn't he?'

'Is the clothing that he washed still here?'

'He took it to his mum's when he left yesterday.' She ping-ponged her gaze between Barry and Hunter, then threw up her hands to her mouth. 'This is about that attack on the woman on the Craggs, isn't it? Oh my God!'

Barry went over to her and put his hand on her shoulder. 'It's something we're following up, Kim. Dylan's name has been mentioned but it might not be anything.'

Kim shook her head in disbelief.

'Is it okay if we have a look around? We just want to check Dylan's things.'

'But I already said, he took the things he washed to his mum's yesterday.'

'Does he have anything else of his here? I believe he lives with you?'

'He's got some stuff here. Mainly clothes. They're upstairs in the bedroom.'

'Do you mind if we have a quick look?'

Kim nodded.

The bedroom was a good size, containing a double bed, two bedside cabinets, a set of drawers and fitted wardrobes. The wall behind the bedhead was papered with floral design wallpaper. The other three walls had been painted dark red.

'Which side does Dylan sleep at?' Barry asked.

Kim pointed to the left side of the bed and Barry walked over to the bedside cabinet.

'You check the wardrobes, Hunter,' Barry said, pulling open the top drawer.

The fitted wardrobes had four doors and Hunter opened one of them. Seeing it was filled with Kim's clothes, he closed it and opened the one next to it. That also contained Kim's clothes. The third door he opened contained Dylan's and he started rooting through.

This wardrobe wasn't as tidy as Kim's. There were some t-shirts and shirts neatly hung on hangers, together with a pair of jeans, but a lot of the clothing lay clustered at the bottom. It was those items that Hunter chose to go through first, instantly noting that the majority of the stuff was soiled and in need of washing and he put on his gloves to sift through.

He picked each item up carefully, gave it the once-over and placed it behind him on the carpet. He had taken out most of the things, and was nearing the bottom of the washing, when he spotted something small and dark, rolled up. He picked it up with a finger and thumb, catching his breath as it unfolded. Holding it up in front of his face, he called out, 'Barry!' and spun around to reveal a black woollen ski mask.

CHAPTER SIXTEEN

Kim Davies had not slept. Even though PC Kerr had assured her that the night shift would make regular passing patrols, she had become a nervous bundle the moment they had left her flat. She knew that Dylan would blame her for this even though she'd had nothing to do with it. Once they had gone she had secured the door as best she could, even wedging a chair under the handle for extra security — she'd seen it done on the telly — but it had not helped her sleep. She'd twice heard a car below her window and peeked out through the curtains. It was a police car, as promised, and yet she still felt uneasy. Finally, as dawn broke, and realising sleep was still a long way off, she slipped on her kimono and made her way downstairs to the kitchen to make herself a coffee.

At the bottom of the stairs she paused and gazed in the hallway mirror. Her reflection was not a pretty sight. Rheumy, panda-like eyes stared back. Taking a step nearer, she pulled aside the collar of her kimono and viewed the ugly marks Dylan had left behind on her neck. She delicately traced a finger around the tender swelling. It was beginning to bruise. Her scalp was sore as well where he had yanked out chunks of her hair. A tear formed in the corner of an eye. She blinked it away. How had she put it with his behaviour for so long? Her friends had warned her to dump him but she hadn't.

Suddenly, the clattering of milk bottles outside her door brought her thoughts back. The milkman's here, she thought and began to drag the chair away from under the handle.

Back pressed against a tree, clenching and unclenching his hands, Dylan Wolfe stared up at the flat where his girlfriend lived. He was shaking. Not from the chill of the early morning but from the pent-up homicidal fury rampaging inside.

That bitch had sold him out to the cops and now it was time to make her to pay.

Fixing his angry stare upon the curtained windows of Kim's first-floor flat, thinking through how he could get in there without causing too much fuss, and catch her unawares, the whine of an electric milk float going towards the block suddenly gave him an idea.

He launched himself away from the tree and broke into a jog.

Slowing his pace, waiting for the milkman to enter by the main doors, Dylan caught the door before it fastened behind. He entered the ground floor hallway to see the milkman beginning his climb to the first floor.

'I'll take that, mate,' Dylan said in a low voice, holding out a hand.

The milkman turned and with a recognising look said, 'I don't normally see you at this time in the morning.'

'Got a new job. Been on nights this week. Soon be tucked up in a warm bed, though.'

The milkman removed a pint of milk from his wire basket and handed it over.

Dylan mounted the concrete stairs quickly and reaching the landing, he glanced downwards. The milkman had left. Knowing Kim's routine, he chinked the bottle loudly against the wall and stepped to one side.

He heard a shuffle behind the door, followed by the sound of something being dragged. Then he heard the key turn and the safety chain being unlatched.

A tingling sensation coursed through his body, and crouching into a squat, he tensed.

As the door cracked open, Dylan launched himself. The force of his thrust spiralled Kim backwards, smacking her against the hall wall.

A groan exploded from her mouth as Dylan made a lunge. He made a grab for her short wrap but the satin material slipped through his fingers, and she slid sideways to the floor, throwing him off balance. He stumbled against the stairs, catching his head against the bottom post and let out a moan.

Kim let out a piercing scream.

'Shut up, you fucking bitch!' he yelled and lashed out with a foot. It caught the top of her arm. He pulled back his foot again, but before he could deliver the second kick, Kim shot up her leg and flat-footed his groin.

It was his turn to groan as he instantly doubled-up, grabbing at his testicles.

Scrambling backwards on all fours, trying to lift herself up, Kim clambered into the kitchen. Recovering quickly, and heaving himself forward, Dylan followed, pain and hate cascading through him. He entered the kitchen just as Kim was attempting to pull herself up. Beyond her fingers he spotted a glint of metal on the work surface. At the same time, he caught the movement in Kim's eyes. She was following his gaze and had locked onto the same thing he had clocked.

Her face took on a look of horror as he propelled forward.

Kim only had time to scream 'NO' once, before Dylan plunged the kitchen knife into her chest.

At 6.25 am, Hunter finally gave up hope of trying to get to sleep and excitedly leapt from his bed to get a shower; the previous evening, after failing to locate Dylan Wolfe, the inspector had told him that his day off had been cancelled, and he was to report back that morning to work with Barry and the team investigating the attacks on Elizabeth Barnett and Anita Thompson and track Dylan down.

He had sped home from the station and burst into his home unable to hold back from telling his parents the news that he was working with CID. They had been so pleased for him, and quizzed him about the case, especially his mother. The buzz had coursed through him the whole of last night; he had been unable to concentrate, even on watching his favourite TV show, The Bill, and in bed, he had tossed and turned, his head full of all manner of exciting stuff. Three months into his probation he was working with CID on a major investigation. It couldn't get any better.

Towelling himself dry, he dressed in the dark grey suit he had worn for his police interview, matching it with a light blue Oxford button-down shirt and dark blue and white striped tie. As he tightened the tie into his collar, he gave himself the once-over in the mirror, telling himself that at least he looked the part, even if he couldn't compete with his CID colleagues. He grabbed a piece of toast and a cup of tea, which he bolted down, and then drove hurriedly into work, thinking about what the day ahead was going to bring.

Hunter was the first in the Investigation Teams Office and he ran his eyes over the incident board. As he studied and absorbed the timeline of events, an overwhelming sense of elation suddenly enveloped him as it dawned on him that he was now part of this enquiry — and so early on in his career. He couldn't have dreamed this up.

'Shit the bed, Hunter?'

Barry's gruff voice caused him to turn. 'Couldn't sleep, Barry,' he replied, casting his gaze upon him. Barry looked as untidy as ever. His dark mop of curly hair was ruffled, his thick bushy moustache was desperately in need of a trim, his dark blue tie hung haphazardly from his unfastened collar and his grey slacks were in need of a press.

Barry let out a short laugh. 'I remember looking as smart as you once upon a time. Anyway, Hunter, your job first thing is to stick the kettle on and make us both a brew. I spoke with the DI last night before I went off — you're partnering me today to find Dylan. You okay with that?'

'Certainly am,' Hunter answered elatedly.

'Good man.'

Hunter had just filled the kettle and switched it on when one of the phones rang.

Barry snatched it up. 'DC Newstead, CID.' He had been on the phone for less than twenty seconds, listening, not speaking, when he slammed down the handset and shouted to Hunter, 'That cuppa's gonna have to wait. They've just had a three-nines. Kim Davies has been stabbed.'

By the time Hunter and Barry got to 18 Dearne View the complex was teeming with uniform and an ambulance was just arriving.

Hunter and Barry stormed through the entrance doors and took the stairs two at a time up to the first floor, where they found the door to Kim's flat wide open.

Hunter spotted a bloodied handprint on the jamb.

Barry called out loudly, 'Police!' as he jogged into the hallway.

'Through here,' a female voice shouted back.

Barry and Hunter followed the sound along the hall and found a scene of carnage in the kitchen. Blood was spattered all over the cupboards and a thick pool of dark blood surrounded an unconscious woman.

Beneath the bloodied mess, Hunter recognised Kim Davies.

Cradling her was a dark-haired woman in a dressing gown. She too was covered in blood and had a towel pressed over Kim's chest. Glancing up, she said, 'I'm a nurse. I live downstairs. I heard her screaming. She's lost a lot of blood.'

'The ambulance has just arrived,' Barry replied, kneeling down. 'Is there anything we can do?'

'No, I need to keep the pressure on this wound. Her pulse is weak and slow.' Lifting her eyes, the nurse shook her head. She gave a look which said, 'It's touch and go.'

Pushing himself up, Barry met the nurse's gaze. 'Try and keep her with us. I'll go get the ambulance crew.' As he reached the doorway, he looked back. 'You didn't see who did this by any chance, did you?'

'That boyfriend of hers! He nearly knocked me back down the stairs running away.'

In the distance Hunter picked up the sound of wailing sirens. More troops had arrived.

Within half an hour of the attack, uniform and detectives had converged upon Dearne View, swarming around the three tenement blocks, searching for evidence and seeking witnesses. This was Hunter's first practical introduction to preserving a major crime scene and he took in every instruction Barry gave, watching his colleagues secure Kim Davies's flat with tape, extend it down the stairs to the entranceway, and out to the parking area in front of the block, while he took on sentry duties at Kim's door with instructions that he wasn't to let anyone pass other than the forensic team. Then Barry left him to go and brief the officers who had come to assist.

Three-quarters of an hour later the first SOCO officers arrived. There were two. One was a man in his early 40s, rake-thin, with straggly, straw-coloured hair, and the other was a slim woman in her late 20s with short blonde hair, carrying a metal camera case. The man introduced himself as Duncan Wroe and the young woman as Emma Russell. The first question Duncan asked was who, and how many, had been inside the flat following the attack. Hunter told him.

Duncan pointed to the bloody hand mark on the doorframe and turned to his colleague. 'Emma, can you take a shot of that for me? I'm going inside.'

Emma nodded, setting down her camera case and opening it up. It took her just five minutes to set up her tripod and camera and Hunter stepped to one side as she took several photographs. Then she folded it, picked it up, offered him a quick smile and disappeared into the flat.

Less than 20 minutes after that, Barry returned and in tow was PC Steve Turnbull from the dayshift group. Steve Turnbull was just out of his probation and Hunter acknowledged him with a nod.

'Right, Hunter, Steve here is going to take over the door. You and I have more important tasks in hand. Catching Dylan Wolfe for one.' Before Hunter could respond, Barry shouted over his shoulder into the flat, 'You got anything in there for me?'

'Despite you ruining my crime scene with your size elevens, we're getting there.'

Hunter recognised the voice of Duncan Wroe calling back.

Barry issued a snort and replied, 'Keeps you on your toes, Duncan.' Then he dipped his head towards Hunter, 'Come on, we've got a fugitive to catch.'

As Hunter bounded down the steps after Barry, he suddenly felt a sense of importance. Until today, all he had been used for was guarding a scene and doing some door-knocking for witnesses. Now he was at the forefront of a manhunt.

By mid-afternoon, Scenes of Crime had completed a full forensic search of Kim's flat, recovering numerous exhibits, and officers searching the tenements complex had dropped lucky; beneath a drain cover they had recovered a bloodied kitchen knife and it looked like the one missing from the knife block in Kim's flat.

News from the hospital was not so good. Kim had suffered seven stab wounds, all to the chest. One of the wounds had missed her heart by centimetres but had punctured her lung, leaving her with breathing difficulties, thus making surgery precarious. She had been in the operating theatre for four hours and during that time 12 units of blood had been used to keep her alive. She was now on life support in intensive care in a critical state. They had been told that the next 24 hours were crucial to her survival.

Hunter and Barry had done a lot of foot-slogging in their attempts to track down Dylan Wolfe but had little success to show for their endeavours; Dylan's mother told them she hadn't seen him since the previous afternoon when he had left to go to the pub. They got the name of the pub from her and visited it and the landlord confirmed that Dylan had been in there until early the previous evening but had left following a phone call. Barry asked after the caller, but the landlord told them he hadn't a clue. He said it was a young male, but told them that as soon as the caller had asked for Wolfy, he had brought the phone through to the bar and left him to take the call while he served a customer. The next time he had looked, Dylan Wolfe had gone.

Their next point of call was his place of employment. That was a breakers yard at Kilnhurst, where he stripped accident damaged cars for parts to sell. The owner was a burly man in his early 60s with wispy, thinning grey hair and a bald crown. They found him in one of the garages removing the engine from a smashed-up Mercedes. Talking to him had been like pulling teeth, though they did find out that Dylan hadn't been into work for the last two days, but little else. He wasn't forthcoming about his whereabouts and when they asked if they could check his locker they were told 'not unless they had a warrant'. Barry told him in no uncertain terms they would be back and they left.

On the way back to their car, Barry turned to Hunter and said, 'Remember Anita Thompson mentioning that her attacker smelled of oil?' He thumbed back at the breakers yard. 'Well, my guess is that's the reason why. I'm more than confident he's our brace-and-bit burglar, as well as being wanted for attempt murder and rape. Once we finally get him, Dylan Wolfe is going away for a very long time.'

They got into the car and Barry set off slowly, doing his best to avoid the largest of the potholes in the dirt road as he headed back to the station. Pulling on to the main road, he said, 'What about this guy of yours who told you about Dylan?'

Hunter gave him a sideways gaze. 'What about him?'

'Well, do you think he might have an idea where he is?'

'I doubt it. He wasn't even sure of his full name. He only knew him as Wolfy. He'd seen him when he'd been drinking in the Stute.'

'This snout of yours drinks in the Stute?'

Hunter gave a sharp nod. 'I don't know how regular he is there. He seemed to know that Wolfy went in there with his mum and girlfriend when he told me about him.'

'Do you think we could go and have a word with him?'

'I'm not sure how receptive he would be. He's not a lover of cops. He only told me about Wolfy because he owed me one.'

'Can you tell me who this guy of yours is?'

'I don't know. After he'd told me about Wolfy, he said he'd paid back the favour and he didn't want to get involved anymore.'

'You can tell me his name, Hunter. I'm not going to go around pinching anyone's snout. I'm just interested in who gave you the info.'

Hunter thought about it a moment and quickly came to the conclusion that he could trust Barry. He answered, 'George Hudson.'

Barry whipped his head sideways. 'Jud!'

Hunter nodded.

Barry returned his eyes to the road. 'Fuck me, Hunter. Jud gave you the info about Wolfy?'

'Yes.'

'That's a first. As long as I've known Jud, and I've locked him up a few times, he's never squealed on anyone. You must have had something good on him.'

Hunter told him about the incident with the stolen copper boilers from the derelict houses.

Barry gave a sharp laugh. 'Well, good on yer, Hunter. That's sharp practice, that is. If we collar Wolfy thanks to your hold over Jud, this will see you easily through your probation. And it'll mean a commendation. I think that's a fair return.' Barry started tapping the steering wheel, a huge grin playing over his mouth. 'You need to use this to your advantage, Hunter. What

Jud doesn't know about what goes on in this town isn't worth knowing. Talk to him at every opportunity. He could well be your passage into CID in the future.'

Evening briefing provided a mixed bag of information; Kim Davies was still very ill and sedated, although her condition had stabilised and doctors were hopeful of an improvement. And they had achieved success when they had turned over the breaker's yard. In Dylan Wolfe's locker they had found his toolbox and among his work tools they had found an old-fashioned carpenter's hand brace with numerous bits, together with a pair of bloodstained washing-up gloves and a pair of woman's panties, which fitted the description of those taken from Anita Thompson; it was strong enough evidence to link him to her rape.

They had also discovered numerous stolen vehicle parts in the yard and the disgruntled owner was now banged up, waiting to be interviewed by Stolen Vehicle Squad. Frustratingly, though, they hadn't found Dylan Wolfe, despite a full search of his workplace and every known associate and family member being visited.

The best snippet came last of all; Dylan's association with Barnwell Working Men's Club and Institute had delivered dividends: the Stute had also been the regular drinking venue for June Waring and her pals. It was a tenuous link at the moment, but it had the detective inspector very excited and he was assigning some of the murder team onto the hunt for Dylan Wolfe.

CHAPTER SEVENTEEN

Hunter awoke the next morning with a thick head. Following yesterday's briefing, Michael Robshaw, the DI, had taken him to one side and thanked him for his help in identifying Dylan Wolfe as their main suspect and told him that his contribution was being rewarded with an early and extended attachment to CID, commencing Monday. He was told to take his weekend off and enjoy himself. He caught up with Barry in the George and Dragon pub, along with all the rest of the investigation team, and he garbled out his news without taking a breath.

Barry returned a short laugh. 'I know, Hunter. It was me who had a word in the DI's ear. You've earned it. You've had more collars than anyone in CID these couple of months, and it's not bad when a woodentop, and a probationer one at that, comes up with the main suspect in a murder, attempt murder, rape and an aggravated burglary, before us detectives.'

Hunter had locked eyes with Barry. 'Are CID pissed off with me?'

'Not at all. There'll be some who are envious, but the majority, and I include myself, and the DI, will see potential CID material. No, you carry on what you're doing. This is a great start to your career.'

Those words had made for Hunter's night, and in the exhilaration of the moment, he had drunk far more than normal. He had staggered the two miles home, twice throwing up in the roadside and now was regretting it — particularly because he was picking Beth up later that afternoon and he had promised to be at Andy Sharpe's transfer celebration tonight.

When he finally forced himself out of bed and into the shower, he stayed longer than normal, and after drying himself, still feeling crap, he dressed lazily in a sweatshirt and jeans before making his way downstairs.

Jock was waiting for him in the kitchen holding a tumbler half-filled with a frothy, milky yellow concoction. He handed it to him with the words, 'Drink that, son, it'll do ye the world of good. I heard ye fall in last night.'

Hunter returned a sheepish look and took the glass, eyeing it cautiously. 'What is it?'

'Don't ask, just drink it. You'll thank me in a couple of hours.'

Eyeing it a second time, Hunter took a deep breath and swallowed it in one gulp. Halfway down, he gipped, almost bringing the contents back up but somehow managed to keep them down. As he finished the glass, he shuddered. 'God, that was awful.'

'My Da used to give me the same. Works every time.'

'What was it?' Hunter grimaced, placing the empty glass in the sink.

'Raw egg, Alka Seltzer and a wee dram.' After a pause, Jock asked, 'Now what were you celebrating.'

Hunter told him his news and Jock placed a hand on his shoulder. 'Well done, son, I'm proud of yer. Yer mam's away at the shops, but she'll be pleased to hear yer news when she comes home.' Then he turned and snatched up his kit bag. 'Now, I'm away to the gym. If you feel like a session to sweat some of that alcohol out of ye, I'm there until three.'

Hunter acknowledged with a nod. 'Thanks, but I think I'll give it a miss. I'm going to grab something to eat and then clean my car. I'm picking Beth up later and then we're off to a do.'

'Burning the candle at both ends, eh, lad?' Jock chortled as he left.

Hunter made himself some toast and a brew and then cleaned his car. When he had finished, it was as shiny as the day it had come off the forecourt, and after checking the oil and water, he went inside and put on the telly to watch the football scores come in.

By mid-afternoon, he had recovered sufficiently enough to eat something substantial and his mum cooked him a full breakfast, which he devoured hungrily. Then he returned to the football results, dozing on the sofa for half an hour in between checking the scores.

By 5 o'clock he was raring to go, buoyed by the fact that his beloved Sheffield United had turned in a good result against Aston Villa, beating them 2-0. Showering, he put on a shirt and jeans, grabbed his car keys, and bounded downstairs, shouting cheerio to his parents as he left the house.

Outside the weather had taken a turn; it had started to rain and the wind had picked up, stinging his face as he dashed to his car. By the time he'd got to Beth's house the rain had turned to sleet and it was bitterly cold. Beth greeted him, wearing a pink v-neck pullover and a pair of tight black jeans that showed off her shapely long legs. Her blonde hair hung loose on her shoulders and her make-up showed off her sparkling blue eyes and soft lips.

'You look lovely,' said Hunter.

'Thank you.'

'Do you fancy grabbing something to eat before we go to the do?'

'I'm not really that hungry, but you can if you want. But before we go, my mum and dad want to meet you.'

'Oh.'

'Don't say it like that. They're lovely. They only want to see what you're like. I've told them all about you.'

Hunter felt slightly anxious as he followed Beth into the hallway. He hadn't anticipated this.

Beth showed Hunter into the lounge where there was a blazing open fire. Her dad was in an armchair and her mother on the sofa. Her dad immediately turned down the sound of the TV as Beth introduced him. Ray, her father, was the same size as Hunter — 6' 2" — but muscular, with good solid shoulders, and had dark hair that was shorter than his. He remembered that Beth had told him he was the leading fireman on his watch. In Sandra — Beth's mum — he saw an older version of her daughter, instantly noting where Beth got her looks and figure from. He knew that Sandra was a primary school teacher.

Hunter took up the spare place on the sofa and succumbed to a series of questions, mainly from Sandra, about his job as a policeman. Whilst he started answering with a nervous flutter in his stomach, within a couple of minutes it was gone, and he told them all about the recent cases he had been involved in and couldn't wait to slip in that he was starting his attachment with CID on Monday.

'Oh, wow, you have done well, haven't you?' said Sandra.

As Hunter nodded, Beth interrupted, 'That's enough, Mum, you'll put him off me.'

'Oh, I'm sure I won't,' Sandra answered back with a smile.

Hunter caught a twinkle in her eye — the same sparkle Beth had, and he jokingly answered, 'I've suffered worse grilling's than this,' and rose from the sofa.

Beth announced, 'Mum, we're off to one of Hunter's colleague's dos. I don't know what time it finishes, but I shouldn't be in late. Don't wait up.' Then she stepped across, gave her mum a peck on the cheek and grabbed Hunter's hand. 'Come on, we don't want to be late.'

As they reached the front door, Hunter whispered, 'Thanks for rescuing me.'

Beth let out a short laugh, then said, 'Parents.'

Andy Sharpe's leaving do was in the George and Dragon. The landlord was a retired cop who once worked the beat at Barnwell and was one of the reasons why the place was a magnet for local cops. The other reason was that it was a regular place for a lock-in. Tonight was going to be no exception; the landlady was putting on some food and a couple of officers had brought along their guitars for a sing-song once the regular punters had left.

Hunter led Beth into the pub. It was rammed. Andy Sharpe was at the bar just getting in a round and Hunter saw his shift colleagues crammed around a couple of tables to his left. Also at the bar, he spotted Barry, together with John Vickers and a couple of detectives from the investigation team. He nodded to acknowledge them but decided not to approach Barry — he would have three weeks of his time from Monday. The feeling of excitement was still surging through him.

'What do you want to drink?' he asked Beth.

'Half a lager, please.'

Hunter squeezed between a couple of regulars, sidling up next to Andy who was piling a round of drinks onto a tray.

Andy turned with the drinks, noticing Hunter. 'Hi, Hunter. A little bird tells me you're going into CID on Monday.'

Hunter felt himself going red. 'It's only my attachment, Andy. They've brought it forward because of all these jobs.'

'You've turned up their main suspect, this Dylan Wolfe guy, I'm told.'

Hunter nodded.

'Well, congratulations. CID might come to you earlier than you thought, if you carry on like this.'

'Thanks, Andy. I've got my fingers crossed. It'd be nice if I could get in on his arrest. That would put me in good standing. And that reminds me to congratulate you again on getting into traffic. I know you've dreamed of this for a while.'

'Five years.'

'Hope I'm not waiting five years.'

'I'm sure you won't. And thanks again. I know it's only been a short time, but I've enjoyed working with you. You've got the makings of being a good cop.'

'It's been a pleasure working with you as well, Andy. You've scared the shit out of me on more than one occasion, but you're the best driver I've known. I've learned a lot from you.'

'Thanks, Hunter.' Andy started to push past him, heading to the tables where his shift was, but then paused and leaned into Hunter's ear. 'By the way, no XR2 will get the better of me, just you watch that speed of yours.'

Hunter caught the mischievous smile playing across Andy's mouth and let out a laugh. 'I might just give you a run for your money one day.'

Andy nudged him as he slipped past. 'As if,' he replied, and added, 'I'll pull up a couple of chairs, you can introduce your girlfriend to us when you've got your drink.'

Hunter bought himself a pint and half a lager for Beth, and steered her towards the table where his shift colleagues were seated, telling her, 'You'll like them,' as he spotted two empty chairs lined up between Roger and Andy.

For the best part of three hours, Hunter's shift talked and laughed as comrades. They told Beth about the prank they had played on him with the mannequin, causing Hunter to blush, and one by one they revealed funny anecdotes about their colleagues or about incidents they had dealt with. Hunter's sides were aching with some of the stories and he could see Beth was full of laughter as well. As he looked around the table, repeatedly casting his gaze back to Beth, Hunter couldn't help but think what a good career choice he had made and how lucky he had been with meeting Beth. This was fate.

The ringing of the bell at the bar signifying last orders, brought back his thoughts. He had finished his pint, and wanted no more because he was driving and so leaned across to Beth. 'Have you had enough?'

Beth met his gaze and nodded. 'I have, Hunter. I'm on early tomorrow and I don't want to go in smelling of drink. The sister's quite a stickler.'

'Come on then, we'll say our goodbyes and leave.'

When Hunter mentioned to his teammates they were leaving, there were a round of calls, jokingly telling him he couldn't take the pace and he'd never get in CID if he couldn't drink, but Hunter knew it was all in jest and he grabbed his coat, bid them all a goodnight and headed for the door with Beth.

Outside, they were met by a blast of bitter northern air, and the earlier rain and sleet had intensified and was coming down as a thick flurry of snow. Hunter shivered, surprised by the sudden cold snap, quickly zipping up his coat and hitching up the collar.

'Crikey, brass monkey weather,' Hunter moaned, pulling Beth close.

'I think they've forecast this for the next couple of days.'

'That's all we need. Might be a white Christmas.'

'Lovely, if you don't have to go into work.'

'Tell me about it.' He gave her a squeeze and headed to the car park.

There were about a dozen cars parked up with lots of spaces between them. As he cast his gaze around the car park, he froze. His car wasn't where he thought he'd parked it. He quickly ran his eyes around again. His car definitely wasn't there. He looked to Beth.

She had followed his gaze. 'Your car's not here!'

In that moment he remembered the prank his colleagues had played on him months ago and he rummaged in his pockets for his car keys. He found them where he'd put them, zipped up in the inside pocket of his coat. He scoured the car park again, the realisation rapidly dawning. 'Someone's nicked my car. The bastards.'

CHAPTER EIGHTEEN

Sunday morning dawned and Hunter rolled out of bed, shattered. He had hardly slept a wink again. This time he was worrying about his car. He was hoping against hope that it had been taken by some teenage toerag, who just wanted to take it for a joyride and then abandon it in one piece. The alloys alone were worth a couple of hundred quid, and on that thought the breakers yard at Kilnhurst popped into his head. He wondered if someone from there had taken it in reprisal for their actions yesterday. He would ring the station and ask the day shift to check it out.

After a quick shower, Hunter rang the nick. Harry Hemsworth answered. He hadn't any good news. The night's duty group had checked all the known dumping sites for stolen vehicles and had found a burned-out motorcycle, but not his car. He thanked Harry, mentioned the breakers yard, and put down the handset, feeling disappointed.

'No use moping, son,' said Jock, appearing in the kitchen doorway. 'That's not going tae get it back any sooner. Why not get yourself some breakfast, and then come down with me to the gym and take it out on the punchbag?'

Hunter thought about it for a few seconds and then agreed; moping around the house wasn't going to change anything, and Beth was on days, so he wouldn't be seeing her today.

His parents had already breakfasted, so he made himself some toast, while Fiona mashed a pot of tea, and then after bolting it down, he placed his dirty pots in the sink and nipped upstairs for his gym kit.

Jock drove them there, getting in the dig that if he'd have bought the Volvo it wouldn't have got nicked, which Hunter responded to by making a disgruntled growl, bringing a belt of laughter from Jock.

At the gym, Hunter pushed some weights, did some skipping, and thumped the punchbag for a good quarter of an hour, and then ended his training session sparring in the ring with Jock. He was soaked by the time he had finished and although his car was still in his thoughts, he didn't feel as troubled about it.

Hunter showered, and slipping into jeans and a sweat top, he made himself and Jock a cuppa and took it to him ringside. There were half a dozen people working out in the gym — all young men — among them a couple of Jock's boxing protégés and Jock was watching one of them go through his paces with one of the trainers.

Jock took the mug of steaming tea from Hunter, passing him a quick glance, before returning his eyes back to the bigger than average 15-year-old sparring with the trainer. 'He's got the makings of a good fighter,' said Jock.

Hunter watched Jock's shoulders and neck going in time with the punches being thrown by the young boxer in the ring and smiled to himself. He knew Jock had been a good boxer in his time — the Commonwealth Medal was testimony to that — but he also knew from watching him train, and from doing some sparring work with him, that he still had a lot of agility and could throw one hell of a punch for a 40-year-old. He wouldn't fancy going toe to toe with him like he'd done with Matty Smith, the burglar.

Jock turned to him. 'Anyway, what are you up to for the rest of the day? Got any plans? I lock up here at one, if you fancy going for beer?'

Hunter thought about it for a moment, then replied, 'No thanks, Dad. Do you know what, I think I'm going to nip round and see Polly's parents. I keep promising I'll call in and I haven't done since I joined the police.'

'I think they'll like that, son. Me and yer ma bumped into them down the shops and they were asking how you were going on.'

Polly's parents, Geoff and Lynn Hayes, lived in a 1960s semi, a quarter of a mile from Hunter's own home. Geoff answered the door, and his face lit up when Hunter told him, he'd just popped round to see them.

Calling out, 'Guess who's come to see us,' Geoff ushered him quickly into the lounge, where Lynn was sitting on the sofa.

'Sit yourself down, Hunter,' Geoff said, pointing out the space next to his wife, and made his way to an armchair.

Geoff and Lynn, like Hunter's parents, were also in their early 40s, though, as he eyed them both, he thought they looked to have aged far more than his parents and couldn't help but think that Polly's death was responsible for that.

Geoff was an engine driver on the railways and Lynn worked in the Post Office. Hunter had spent quite a bit of time in their company when he had dated Polly and got on very well with them. When she had first been murdered, and he had been taken to the police station as a suspect, he had stayed away, but weeks after her funeral, they had appeared at his home one evening, telling him that they knew he wasn't responsible and begging him to call and see them. And so he had done, and he had been so glad, because they had shared many fond memories with him. More so than when she had been alive.

When he had told them he wasn't going to art college and was joining the police service instead, they had been as surprised as his parents by the news. Just before he had gone to training school, he had called in to see them, promising he would call in regularly and keep them updated. It hadn't been necessary to explain what he was going to keep them updated about, the look on their faces had told him they understood. However, since being posted, he had been so caught up in his work, he had neglected to call on them.

As he plonked himself down beside Lynn, he suddenly felt a shred of guilt, particularly when he set his eyes on the last school photo of Polly, which took centre-stage on the mantelpiece alongside the holiday snaps of her. *I'll catch your killer Polly*, he thought, *if it's the last thing I do.*

For the next hour, the three of them went back over old memories and though he could relate to her school antics because he had known her all through school, he was lost when mention of their holidays came around. Hunter had never been on holiday with the Hayes, but did know that since Polly had been five, as a family they had gone camping each year in Cornwall. She had gone two months after they had started going out together and had written to him three times during that holiday telling him about what she was up to and ending each one with how much she was missing him and that she couldn't wait to get back home to see him.

Tragically, a month after receiving those letters Poly had been killed and, thankfully, he still had them as a memory of their short time together. They were currently in a shoebox at the top of his wardrobe together with a couple of photographs of her.

The conversation drifted naturally towards himself and they started to ask him about his job. They wanted to know how he'd got on at training school, how he was getting on with his colleagues and asked him if he'd been involved in any of the jobs that they'd seen on the news. When he told them he had, they wanted to know more and Hunter eagerly divulged the leading part he'd played.

'So you know who's done all these attacks?' Lynn asked.

Hunter nodded. 'I'm going into CID tomorrow for three weeks to help try and catch him.'

'Can you tell us who it is?' Lynn probed.

'Sorry, I'm not allowed to tell anyone at the moment. All I'll say is that I don't think you'll know them.'

'That's all right, Hunter, we understand.' Geoff tapped his nose.

'I'll pop in and tell you all about it after we've caught him.'

'Promise?' said Lynn.

Hunter nodded. 'Promise.'

There was a short pause and then Geoff said, 'We bumped into your mum and dad the other day when we were out shopping.'

'Yes, Dad told me.'

'It was good to see them again. Your mum said you'd got a new girlfriend.'

Hunter felt himself colouring up and suddenly he felt uncomfortable. 'Er, yes.'

'We don't want to embarrass you, Hunter. It's only natural you'll find a new girlfriend. You're still very young. Polly would want you to move on. She'd be horrified if you didn't.'

Hunter nodded awkwardly. He wanted this part of the conversation to move on. To take it in another direction, he said, 'Did my dad tell you about my car?'

'He did. A red sporty one, he said,' Geoff answered with a sharp burst of laughter. 'I remember my first car, a ropy old

Vauxhall Viva. It was in the garage more than on the road. Not like that these days. What make is it?'

Hunter told him and added, 'It was nicked last night.'

'What, your car was stolen?' Lynn gasped, throwing her hand up to her mouth.

'Do you know who's taken it?' asked Geoff.

'Not yet I don't, but when I do, he's in for it.'

Geoff laughed. 'Taking a copper's car is not a good move, eh?'

'Not good at all,' Hunter answered with a mischievous smile. 'Well, I'm going to get off home now and check in if they've found my car, if that's okay.'

Hunter rose, and Geoff and Lynn followed his action.

Lynn said, 'It's lovely to see you again, Hunter. I'm so pleased to hear how you're getting on.'

'And I wish you well with CID tomorrow. Hope you get your man,' added Geoff.

'So do I,' said Hunter.

Geoff opened the front door for him, reaching out to shake Hunter's hand. Hunter took it. For a second, Geoff held on to his hand and Hunter thought he caught tears welling up in Geoff's eyes.

Letting go of Hunter's hand, Geoff said, 'And don't be a stranger, Hunter. You know where we are. Please keep in touch.'

'I will,' answered Hunter, feeling a lump emerge in his throat.

As Hunter set off down the path, he felt a degree of sadness. He liked Geoff and Lynn, and he couldn't help but wonder how things might have been had he still been dating Polly. One thing he was certain of was that was he was pleased he'd gone and seen them. It was one demon he had exorcised.

CHAPTER NINTEEN

It was early evening. Slightly built, 61-year-old Efrat Gurmani was small against most men, but what he lacked in stature he made up with his strength of character. Efrat always wore a pleasant smile for his customers and was very obliging. He was working on his shop floor, replenishing the booze on the shelves because there was a lull. He was currently running an offer on cans of strong lager and large bottled cider and it was proving popular. He had just opened a box of bottled lager when two men crashed in through the door, bringing with them a flurry of snow. One of them was yelling something, and at first, because they were wearing Santa masks, he thought it was some kind of stunt, until he saw the gun pointing straight at his face. He froze.

'Give us the fucking money!' the one with the gun shouted.

The other one was standing by the door, his Santa face jerking back and forth, keeping lookout. Efrat saw he was holding a knife.

'Don't do anything stupid. This gun is fucking real.'

Efrat slowly straightened, holding up his hands in surrender. 'No problem, I give you money. Don't hurt me. I am family man.'

The one with the gun grabbed him by his cardigan and pushed him towards the counter.

'Open the fucking till,' the man yelled in Efrat's ear. 'Do anything stupid and you're fucking dead. Understand?'

Efrat nodded. The gunman still held onto Efrat as he lifted the counter and stepped behind it. Then the man let go of Efrat's cardigan. Efrat watched him turn his head towards his accomplice and that's when he made his decision. He'd already been robbed twice and he had worked far too hard to let two more scumbag druggies take his money. He wrapped his fingers around the edge of the baseball bat he kept propped near the till and, snatching it up, he swung it over his head. The bat snagged on the ceiling Christmas decorations, dragging them down as it arced towards the gunman's mask. That snagging jolted his arm and Efrat missed the man's head by inches.

The gunman jumped back, firing off a shot.

Efrat flinched, ducking to one side. He heard something whistle past his ear and hit the wall behind him. He raised the bat again for a fresh swing and another shot rang out. He felt something sting his left arm, throwing him back against the cigarette cabinet. He dropped the bat, grabbing the upper part of his arm. Looking down, he saw blood seeping through his cardigan. As he lifted his gaze, his legs buckled and he slumped to the floor on his backside.

The gunman leapt through the opening. 'Stupid fucking Paki!' he screamed, pointing the gun at Efrat's head.

Efrat thought that this was where his life ended and closed his eyes, but after two seconds, when there was no gunshot, he snapped them open. The gunman had keyed his till and was rifling through it, stuffing notes into his pockets. Efrat's arm was burning. His chest tightened and he found himself gasping for breath. Then, without warning, an explosion of stars erupted behind his eyes and everything started to blur.

In the Barnwell police station locker room, Hunter ran a hand over his dark brown hair and studied his reflection in the mirror. The dark blue suit Beth had helped him choose yesterday was perfect. He thought he looked like a detective already. He was also pleased with the new buzzcut he had acquired; it was all the fashion, and for the short time he was out of uniform, he could get away with wearing it like this.

Taking a step back, he checked that the Windsor knot in his tie was tight to the collar, straightened his jacket, ran his eyes over his well-polished shoes and, happy with his appearance, made his exit.

As he took the flight of steps up to the CID department, he wondered what the evening ahead might hold; Barry had rung his home the previous day to tell him that it looked like Dylan Wolfe had well and truly gone to ground and that he and Hunter had been designated enquiries to visit the local pubs and clubs in the area to see if they could get a lead on his whereabouts.

That task meant they were to work 6 pm until 2 am. It had given Hunter additional time to sort out his car insurance and transport, following the theft of his XR2. He was still seething and couldn't wait to get his hands on the culprit who'd nicked it. He had already determined he was going to call on George Hudson for help, remembering what Barry had said about Jud knowing most about what was going on in the area. He'd also see if Jud had heard anything about Dylan. Two birds with one stone.

Entering the office in an eager mood, the first person Hunter encountered was Barry, rifling through the paperwork trays on the detective sergeant's desk. Hunter stopped in his tracks, wondering what Barry was up to. Barry pulled out a set of car keys and, turning to Hunter, a huge grin breaking across his face, he held them aloft as if they were a prize. Hunter instantly knew the significance of Barry's gesture — everyone in the station knew that the DS's car was the cleanest and best looked after and the only time a detective got to use it was when the sergeant wasn't around.

'We've got a job,' Barry announced, picking his jacket off the back of his seat.

'A job?' Hunter replied.

'Robbery. Corner shop on the Tree Estate. Control Room says the owner's been shot.'

This was not what Hunter expected on his first shift. A bolt of nervous energy fizzed through him as he hurried after Barry.

The snow was billowing around the CID car and the roads were starting to crust over, making driving conditions dodgy, and it took Hunter and Barry longer than it should have done to get to the reported heist. Hunter was buzzing. This was his first ever robbery — far more exciting than going around the pubs and clubs to find the whereabouts of Dylan Wolfe. And although robberies weren't rare in Barnwell, robberies with guns were. Especially robberies where a gun had been fired and someone had been shot.

Turning into Hawthorne View, they couldn't miss seeing where the hold-up had taken place — the scene was lit up by whirling blue lights; three beat cars and an ambulance were angled to the kerb, parked in a hurry. Hunter pulled in next to the ambulance.

Hunter got out first, dragging his overcoat around him. The wind-driven snow caught him full on, stinging his face. It was freezing. He looked around. Another hour and the roads are going to be really icy, he thought. Certainly not a night to be chasing after robbers in a car. He dragged his gaze back to the store's front door. The convenience store was one of four shops in a long block. The one next to it was empty, the one after that a hairdresser's and the one at the opposite end was a bookmaker's. The convenience store was the only one with its lights blazing.

Above the shops were four self-contained two-bedroom flats. The block was part of the original council development of a thousand or so buildings, most of them semi-detached houses that made up the locally referred Tree Estate.

'What's that smile for?'

Hunter turned to his partner. 'I'm excited. I've never been to a shooting before.'

'I'm excited too, but you don't see me smiling. There're people watching. You might not be one yet, but try to look like a detective, will you?'

Knowing he'd been chided for his naivety, Hunter immediately straightened his mouth, hiding his exuberance. As he made for the store, he glanced sideways at the big man walking beside him. He couldn't believe his luck when he'd been told his CID attachment was being brought forward. Being told that Barry would be his CID mentor was icing on the cake. Barry was the longest serving detective in Barnwell and Hunter had learned such a lot about him since joining the district. Every cop in the district respected Barry — many wanted to be like him — and every villain feared him. Hunter had experienced that fear three years ago when Barry had grilled him over the murder of Polly. Barry had scared the wits out of him. It was something he was never going to forget.

The uniformed cop on the door was Kieran Mitchell from Rota 3. He acknowledged them with a nod and Hunter noted the surprise look on his face at Hunter's attendance.

'We've been told the owner's been shot,' said Barry.

Kieran nodded. 'In the shoulder. He's been very lucky. The paramedics are just seeing to him. His wife and son are in there as well.'

Kieran opened the door for them and Hunter and Barry stepped into the warmth of the shop.

The first thing Hunter took in was the mess on the floor. Swirls of muddy shoe patterns stained the floor, a miniature artificial Christmas tree was on its side, the plastic pot holding it smashed, its baubles and tinsel spilt. Amongst the spilled decorations were several discarded five-pound notes, some loose change and a few cigarette packets. Hanging from the ceiling was a band of shiny red and gold tinsel.

Behind the counter, another cop from Rota 3, Tom Johnson, was standing guard. He met Hunter's gaze, and Hunter nodded, feeling slightly uncomfortable; being on an opposing rota, he felt as if he was on show and being scrutinised, and thinking about that, he started to focus on what was happening before him. Two paramedics were hunched over the owner, a Mr Gurmani. A thick slash of blood started midway up a metal cabinet behind them and finished where the man lay, half propped against it. He was moaning. Hunter guessed the blood trail was from where Mr Gurmani had slid down after being shot.

'Is he going to be all right?' asked Barry.

One of the paramedics — a woman with spikey black hair — looked over her shoulder. 'It looks like the bullet's passed straight through his upper arm. There's an entry and exit wound. He's lost a fair bit of blood but we've stabilised the bleeding.'

'Can I ask him a couple of questions before he goes to hospital?' Barry said.

'Two men, they rob me. One shot me,' rasped Mr Gurmani in broken English.

The other paramedic, a man in his mid-40s, binding Mr Gurmani's upper arm, shuffled to one side so that Barry and Hunter could get a good look.

Hunter could see that Mr Gurmani didn't look at all well. Despite his toffee-coloured skin, he looked pale and his face was pinched with pain.

'You said two men, Mr Gurmani. Did you get a good look at them?' Barry asked.

Mr Gurmani shook his head and winced, screwing up his face. 'They wear masks. Santa masks. It happened fast. They take money and cigarettes.'

'Sir, we need to get him to hospital,' the male paramedic said. He was gently strapping Mr Gurmani's arm across his chest.

Barry held up his hand. 'Just one more question. I see you have security cameras up, Mr Gurmani. Do you have CCTV?'

Hunter followed Barry's pointing hand to the black camera mounted in the corner behind the counter. He knew that CCTV had been around for a good 10 years, but it was mainly high-risk businesses who installed it. To see it fitted in a corner shop was a rarity and he was excited at the prospect of seeing what had been captured on tape.

Mr Gurmani nodded. 'It upstairs.'

'Two officers are upstairs with Mr Gurmani's wife and son,' interjected Tom Johnson. 'They're looking at the tape now.'

Barry acknowledged with a quick nod and turned to Hunter. 'You go and speak with the son and wife and see what's on the tape and then liaise with SOCO. I'll follow Mr Gurmani to the hospital and we'll catch up there.'

It was after 9 pm before Hunter was done at the scene. He followed Duncan Wroe, the Scenes of Crime officer, out of the shop, as Mr Gurmani's son locked up after them. Seeing the terror still etched on the young man's face as he said goodnight, Hunter felt for him. After all, the son was almost the same age as himself and he wondered how he would feel if it had been his father who had just been shot.

It was still snowing and it had settled; a good two inches lay on the ground. Barry had taken the CID car to the hospital and was still there but thankfully Duncan had agreed to drop Hunter off at Barnwell General, otherwise he would have been stuck. Climbing into the front of the van, he thanked Duncan and told him how grateful he was for the lift.

Hunter checked his watch again and made a mental note of the time. He had been at the store almost three and a half hours. He had been on Duncan Wroe's shoulder a good part of the time, watching him doing a thorough job of examining the scene. The SOCO officer had recovered several sets of the offender's footprints — both had been wearing trainers, and he had taped and recovered glove marks from the counter, till, and metal cigarette cabinet. He had also recovered the remains of two bullets — one from the plasterwork of the wall at the back of the counter, and one from inside the cigarette cabinet, where it had ended up after passing through Mr Gurmani's arm. The bullets casings had been found on the shop floor. Duncan told Hunter they were from a .38 gun — more than likely from a Webley & Scott Enfield pistol used by the British Army during World War Two.

When he hadn't been watching Duncan, Hunter had taken statements from Mr Gurmani's wife and son, who had heard the shots, but neither had seen anything. The son said he had heard a car screech away, but it had gone by the time he'd dashed to the lounge window above the shop.

The VHS tape of CCTV footage Hunter had viewed of the robbery was not much use. Although the entire incident had been captured, it was a cheap system that had been installed and the black and white grainy images could never be used to identify the two offenders.

To compound his lack of success he hadn't had much help from the residents of the flats above the shops. Only one had been home at the time of the robbery, and although he had heard the shots, by the time he had got to his window, the car, the villains had escaped in, had gone a good 50 yards up the road and the swirling snow had obscured his view. All he had been able to describe it as was a small red hatchback, possibly a Ford Fiesta, which had instantly triggered alarm bells in Hunter's head. Although, not a lot to go on by way of evidence, Hunter had that feeling that the robbers were the ones also responsible for stealing his car. The cheeky bastards.

As Hunter gazed out along the snow-covered street, he shook his head — gutted that it might have been his car used in the robbery. An innocent man could have been killed tonight, and all for less than 200 quid in cash and just over a hundred packets of cigarettes and loose tobacco. It was imperative they caught the perpetrators before someone else got hurt.

Duncan Wroe dropped Hunter off at the front of Barnwell General A & E department. It had been a slow and hazardous journey, even though the snowfall had started to ease. Climbing out, Hunter thanked Duncan and watched the SOCO van trundle away. As he stepped towards the automatic doors a sudden draught caught him and within seconds his eyes were watering. He shivered, dabbing his eyes with his coat sleeve. As his vision cleared, he looked at his watch. It was almost quarter to ten. He knew he wouldn't be getting home this side of midnight.

CHAPTER TWENTY

The next morning, in the rear yard of Barnwell Police station, Hunter sat in the driver's seat of the CID car watching the frozen snow slowly melting on the windscreen. It was still too soon to clear the screen with the wipers. He took a deep breath and let it out slowly. It materialised as vapour. Beside him Barry was chuntering — eager to get on. Hunter's car had been found abandoned early that morning by patrolling officers and Barry wanted to check if it was the car used in last night's robbery.

Hunter was eager to go as well — his thoughts centred on what state his car would be in — but he still couldn't see properly out of the screen. Ten minutes earlier those thoughts had just been on getting himself a warm cuppa to thaw himself out after his trudge to the station, but the instant he had stepped into the office, Barry had grabbed him.

'Don't take your coat off, mucker, looks like they've found your car,' Barry had said, throwing Hunter a set of car keys, brushing past him and making for the stairs. 'We're heading towards Goldthorpe.'

The screen finally cleared and Hunter set off. The roads had been ploughed and gritted, but Hunter still drove carefully. In between giving directions, Barry told him that his XR2 had been found an hour ago by Road Traffic along a stretch of country lane. It looked to have skidded off at a bend just before the River Dearne and gone down the banking.

As Hunter took the narrow road towards Goldthorpe, he was already thinking the worst about the state he would find his car in.

Road Traffic was still there when Hunter and Barry arrived. The marked Volvo was parked, half-on, half-off the road, with its hazards blinking. Hunter pulled in behind and got out. Overnight, the temperature had dropped to minus three, crystallising the snow so that it crunched beneath his feet. Stepping cautiously, to avoid slipping, he made his way to the front of the patrol car.

Two officers were sat in the car. As Hunter neared the driver's door, the window powered down. He felt the heat from inside the car the moment he bent to speak with the driver, whom he instantly recognised as Andy Sharpe.

'Hey up, Hunter, hadn't anticipated meeting you so quick. I forgot you were on your attachment.'

'You've found my car, I understand.'

'Afraid so, Hunter. It's just down there,' Andy replied, pointing to the roadside hedge, some of which was ripped out, leaving a gap big enough for a car to get through. 'And it's not in a good state. It looks like the front axle might be damaged. They've gone down the banking and hit a rock. They were very lucky! If they hadn't, they would have ended up in the river.'

'I wish they fucking had.'

Andy let out a short laugh. 'Now, now, Hunter.'

'Anything in the car to suggest it might have been used in our robbery?' Hunter asked, mouth set tight.

'Possibly. There's a couple of packets of cigarettes in the passenger side footwell.'

'Have you touched anything?'

Andy shook his head. 'We left it for you. Just had a quick look inside. Not touched a thing.'

'Great. Thanks.'

'It's been hot-wired. It looks like there might have been three of them. The driver and front passenger door are open as well as the rear passenger door.'

'Okay.'

'Oh, and there's a hole in the windscreen and some specks of blood. I'm no expert but it looks like a bullet hole.' After a pause, Andy added, 'I told you it wasn't good, Hunter. If you ask me, I think the insurance will be writing off your car.' Before Hunter had time to say anything further, Andy said, 'Right, we'll leave it with you then. It's snap time. Good luck.' With that, Andy wound the window back up and the traffic car pulled away from the side of the lane.

'Typical fucking Traffic,' Barry muttered, watching the car disappear around a bend.

Following a set of skid marks in the slush, Hunter and Barry stepped through the large gap torn in the roadside hedge and drew to a halt. They were faced with a steep descent and precarious slippery conditions to where Hunter's XR2 rested at the edge of the riverbank, its front tyres half submerged in lapping icy waters. Hunter picked out several sets of scrambling footprints, trailing up, as well as down, the snowy banking and inwardly sighed; the curiosity of Andy Sharpe and his colleague had contaminated the escaping villain's footprints. It was impossible to see which of the footprints belonged to the cops and which the robbers. He caught the low cursing noise Barry made next to him and knew he was thinking the same.

Hunter lifted his gaze and scoped his surroundings. Snow-covered fields led away from the gentle sweeping riverbank for several miles to the distant low hills of the Dearne Valley. Here the hillside blurred in the blaze of a low horizon, bright, winter sun, which bathed everything in a warm yellow glow. Despite this, Hunter could feel the cold creeping into his body, coming up through the soles of his shoes.

A sudden burst of raucous cawing diverted his attention to a stand of trees to his right where a parliament of rooks had taken flight. A flash of orange grabbed his interest and he saw a fox breaking cover for a few seconds before disappearing again into the undergrowth. Given other circumstances he could have stayed here, exploring this environment for ages. Now though, he and his partner had a job to do, and as he pulled back his look, he could see Barry was already making his way gingerly down the banking.

Spurred into action, Hunter set off after him, his breath leaving his mouth as icy clouds. Keeping a good yard from his abandoned car, Hunter joined Barry by the river edge where he saw that the front end of the car was resting on a good-sized boulder. It was just as Andy Sharpe had said, a rock by the water's edge had prevented it from ending up in the river but at the same time it had buggered up the axle and probably the suspension.

Hunter had a bad feeling about this. Andy's words about the insurance company writing off his car were stuck inside his head. Putting that thought to one side, he dragged his focus back to evidence gathering. Both front doors were open, as was one of the rear passenger side doors. Footprints led away, joining the scramble of others up the banking to the broken section of hedge.

Without touching the car, Hunter and Barry edged around it to the front, watching where they placed their feet — neither of them wanted to end up in the freezing water. As Andy had said, there was a hole in the windscreen, jagged lines radiating away from it and there were signs of blood on the inside. The only time Hunter had seen a bullet hole in glass was in the movies, and this certainly mirrored those images.

He gave Barry an enquiring look, dipping his head towards the damaged screen. 'Think there was an accident? The gun went off when the car crashed?'

'It'd be fucking justice if one of the bastards had shot themselves. We'll need to check with the hospitals but we haven't had a phone call from any of them to my knowledge.' Barry stepped around the open front passenger door, craning his neck inside to take a look. 'It looks like there're spots of blood on the dash as well, but it's not much. Whoever was in the front has certainly had some kind of accident.' He pulled his head back and patted Hunter on the shoulder, 'Sorry to say, Hunter, but I think Andy's right about your car.'

Hunter nodded disconsolately. 'I know he's right. That was my pride and joy.'

'Well, we can always beat the twats up when we catch them.'

Hunter looked at Barry's twisted smile and burst out laughing.

Barry said, 'Come on, we don't want to contaminate the scene any further. We'll call it in and check how long before SOCO get here. It's my guess they'll winch the car up and take it to a drying room to be examined. We ain't going to know anything until at least late on tomorrow.'

Barry began the climb back up to the road and Hunter followed. They had just reached the top when their radios burst into life. It was a request for them to go to The Crescent — a home help assistant had just found one of her clients dead — it looked like he had been shot in the head.

Hunter and Barry exchanged looks with one another and then made a dash for the car.

On the way to the crime scene, Hunter and Barry were updated over the radio. They learned that number 12, The Crescent, was the home of 38-year-old, wheelchair-bound, Derek Vicarage. By the time they got there, two patrol cars and an ambulance were already in attendance and PC Kieran Mitchell was stringing out blue and white police tape between lampposts to seal off the road. Kieran halted setting the cordon to allow them to pass through and then continued with his work.

Hunter and Barry made their way through the gate and down the side of the bungalow to the rear, where they met two paramedics leaning against the wall by the back door. One of them was drawing heavily on a cigarette. The man smoking gazed their way. 'CID?' he enquired.

Barry nodded.

'He's dead. Definitely been shot. Once to the head.' He shook his head. 'Terrible. Who'd want to kill someone who's disabled? What's the world coming to?'

Barry didn't answer, simply flicked up his eyes in disgust as he walked into the kitchen.

Hunter followed.

It was a small kitchen with fitted, tired-looking units, cluttered with foodstuffs and kitchen utensils. To his left, Hunter could hear and see activity through an open door that led into the lounge. He could see a TV was on. As he stepped into the doorway, he caught his first full view of the crime scene. The first thing that hit him was the heat, quickly followed by the reek of piss and shit. He saw that a mounted gas fire was on full. PC Tom Johnson was standing by a man slumped awkwardly in a wheelchair. The victim had his back to them, his head hanging at an angle, blood matting his collar-length dark hair. A pair of spectacles was on the carpet, stuck in the middle of a pool of congealed blood.

Tom Johnson exchanged a smile with Hunter, and said, 'You're certainly making your mark, Hunter. Murder, rape and robbery, all in your first year.'

Hunter returned a smile and said, 'Do you know much about this job?'

'Home help found him just over half an hour ago. She was in a bit of a state when I got here, as you can imagine, so I got Mick Keszeg to take her back to the station and get some more details from her. I've told him to get a statement before she leaves.'

Hunter knew that Mick Keszeg was also on Tom's duty group. He nodded, stepping in front of the victim to get a good view. He saw the distinct mark of a single gunshot to the front of the man's head. He also had a deep gash beneath his left eye. 'Shot once, the paramedic said?'

Tom nodded. 'Looks like that. I haven't touched him but there doesn't appear to be any other blood elsewhere on his body.' He pointed to the man's face. 'It looks as though he's been whacked first. You can see his glasses have been knocked off. You can also smell that he's messed himself.' Pausing, he asked, 'Think it's the same team who did last night's robbery?'

Hunter hunched his shoulders. 'Bit of a coincidence, two people shot on the same night.'

Barry nodded in agreement. 'Does it look as if anything's been taken?'

'The home help woman says he kept some money hidden under his mattress and in a tin in the wardrobe.' Tom chinned towards a door. 'I've had a quick look in his bedroom and his mattress has been disturbed, and it looks as though someone's been through his bedside cupboard and wardrobe. I've closed the door to so that no one goes in before SOCO get here.'

'Good job,' Barry replied. 'Does the home help assistant know roughly how much he keeps around?'

'She told me it could be anything from a few hundred to a couple of thousand. She says she occasionally banks it for him if she sees he's got too much. She says she has warned him loads of times about keeping too much money in the house. She also says he's been warned about letting kids in his house. Apparently, he's a bit of a magnet for teenagers. He buys them booze. He has been visited by social services and given advice in the past.'

'So there's potential for lots of suspects then, as well as witnesses?'

Tom nodded.

Barry turned to Hunter. 'Well, kiddo, you and I better get our sleeves rolled up.'

CHAPTER TWENTY-ONE

That afternoon the CID Office was bustling with activity. The seven detectives who worked the department had been ordered in and each of the desks were taken, so Hunter had to drag a spare chair from the rest room, placing it beside Barry's desk.

The DI, whose office was across the corridor, entered the office, strode to where the filing cabinets were, set down a bundle of loose papers on top of it and unfurled them. Hunter pulled himself up straight and focussed his attention on DI Michael Robshaw, who was casting a glance over his papers, preparing to deliver the briefing.

Robshaw lifted his gaze and said, 'Okay, good afternoon gents, we've got quite a bit of information to go through, so I'm going to cut to the chase and get on with things.' He placed his hand over his paperwork. 'Barry, you've been to both shootings — do you want to take us through the incidents?'

Hunter swung his gaze to his partner, ready to digest and mentally store what his mentor said for when he was in CID.

'First, this morning's murder at number 12, The Crescent,' Barry commenced. 'The victim is 38-year-old Derek Vicarage, who became disabled 10 years ago as a result of an accident down the pit. Mr Vicarage was found by his home help assistant at just after 9 am this morning, dead in his wheelchair, with a single gunshot wound to his head. The pathologist, Professor Graves, said he had been dead at least 12 hours, so that takes us to sometime before 9 pm last night. There was also a nasty cut beneath his left eye, evidence that he had been assaulted prior to his death. There are signs that his bedroom

162

has been searched, and his home help assistant told us that he regularly kept substantial amounts of cash hidden under his mattress and in an old biscuit tin in his wardrobe. SOCO have examined that room and no cash has been found.'

'So we think the motive was probably robbery?' enquired the DI.

Barry nodded. 'Looks that way, Boss. Apparently, it was no secret he had money in the house. The home help assistant told us that social services had paid him several visits because it was known that young people visited him and that he bought them alcohol. And that has been backed up by his neighbours during our house-to-house visits.'

'Do we know the names of those young people?' asked the DI.

Barry shook his head. 'Social Services might know. I've not yet been able to chase that up.'

'That could be why he was killed — he recognised them. Okay, I'll prioritise that as a task. What else did you get from the neighbours?'

'Not much, to be honest. They all knew Derek. Described him as a pleasant man, but because he's a lot younger than them, they have very little to do with him. It was a couple of the neighbours who complained about the young people visiting him because of the noise they made when they left. And one of the neighbours had had some damage done to his garden — his flowers had been pulled up last summer by some of the youths who visited Derek, so they weren't on speaking terms.'

'Anyone hear or see anything yesterday evening?'

Barry again shook his head. 'Except for Derek, they are all pensioners. They lock their doors at night and that is it. None of them were out because of the weather last night. No one heard the gunshot. His immediate neighbours, either side, are hard of hearing.'

'What about post-mortem?'

'Professor Graves is carrying that out this evening. We should know if the bullet that killed Derek is of the same calibre as the ones from the robbery last night.'

'Okay, thanks for that. Now, seeing as you've mentioned it, what about the robbery at the convenience store on Hawthorne Avenue?'

Barry pulled at the loose knot of his tie and cleared his throat again. 'That was just after 5.45 yesterday evening. Two men burst into the store, one wielding a handgun and the other a knife. Mr Gurmani, the owner, describes them both as slim built, wearing jeans and trackie tops. They were wearing Santa Claus masks so he didn't get a look at their faces, but he says they were both white and he thinks they are both young, probably early 20s.

'He said only the one with gun did the talking, mainly shouting at him to hand over the money, and he says it sounded as if he had a local accent. Mr Gurmani keeps a baseball bat behind his counter because he's been robbed twice before and he tried to protect himself by taking a swing at the gunman. That's when he was shot.

'The gunman fired twice. One bullet ended up in the wall behind the counter and the other hit Mr Gurmani in the upper arm. The bullet that hit him went clean through and ended up embedded in the cigarette cabinet. Duncan Wroe from SOCO has recovered both bullets and the casings, and they are both .38. Duncan believes they're from an old World War Two, Webley and Scott Enfield pistol. A lot of servicemen kept them and hid them away as souvenirs and he says that quite a few have ended up in criminal hands over the years.

'I went to the hospital with Mr Gurmani and stayed whilst they operated on him. I spoke with the surgeon after, who said that the bullet had damaged the muscle in his upper arm and he had lost quite a significant amount of blood but they had managed to repair all the damage, and he should make a good recovery once it's healed and he's had some physio. I've rung up the hospital this morning and he's on a ward, where he'll be staying for a couple of days.' Barry looked around at his colleagues. 'I've spoken with the ward nurse who says I should be able to get a statement from him tomorrow.'

'Okay, that's good, Barry. Do we know what was stolen?'

'Mr Gurmani didn't cash up but he thinks there will have been roughly 200 pounds — it was slow yesterday because of the weather. They also got away with some cigarettes, probably around 100 packets and some packets of loose tobacco.'

'Okay, thanks for that, Barry. What about witnesses?'

Barry glanced across at Hunter, pointing at him. 'Hunter spoke with the owner's son and wife and the neighbours in the flat above.'

Clearing his throat, Hunter said, 'Mr Gurmani's wife and son didn't see anything, though they heard the shots. The son heard a car pulling away from the front of the shop but by the time he got to the window it had gone. There is some CCTV evidence but to be honest it's not that much good. Its black and white and the clarity's poor. You can see what went off but it's not good enough for identification purpose.

'As for the neighbours who live in the flats above the shops, only one of the occupants was in at the time of the robbery. He heard the shot, and the car driving away, and was able to describe the car as a red Ford Fiesta, but because of the snow and conditions didn't get a reg number.' Hunter deliberately chose to avoid announcing that it was his car the robbers had used, because he felt embarrassed.

'And we found an abandoned stolen red Fiesta XR 2 this morning, I understand?' Robshaw interjected.

'Traffic did, sir,' Hunter responded, feeling his face warm up. Now he was on the spot. There was no avoiding revealing the truth of the matter. He continued, 'It's actually my car, sir. It was taken from the George and Dragon pub on Saturday evening. It was found down by a section of the River Dearne, on the back road from the Country Park towards Goldthorpe. It looks like they've skidded off the road, probably because of last night's snow. And it does look as if it was the same one used in the robbery. Three of the doors were open and the front passenger side of the windscreen had bullet damage, with some blood on the dashboard and on the inside of the screen. It looks as though the gun has gone off inside the car, probably discharged when they crashed. There is a possibility one of the robbers might have been injured. We have rung Barnwell General but no one was admitted with gunshot wounds. We haven't had time to ring any of the other hospitals.'

'Okay, thanks for that, PC Kerr. And don't feel embarrassed that it was your car. There was nothing you could do about it. It's one of those things. Though I would get a Krooklock after this.' After a short pause, Robshaw asked, 'Anything from SOCO?'

'They've recovered my car and it's been taken to a drying room at Sheffield. They're going to start work on it tomorrow.'

Robshaw rubbed his hands around one another. 'Well, good job, Barry and PC Kerr. We've got a lot to be going on with. I've spoken with the detective super and more resources will be joining us tomorrow. In the meantime, we ring round the hospitals and see if anyone has been brought in with gunshot wounds and we do some more door-knocking around The Crescent. Barry and PC Kerr, I want you two to go to Derek Vicarage's PM this evening.'

Hunter undressed in the darkness of his bedroom, staring out through the window across the garden. It was a full moon and the icy snow shimmered under the moonlight, presenting a soulless, eerie landscape. Unfastening the cuffs of his shirt he pulled it off, smelling the cotton as he confined it to the wash basket. It reeked of that evening's post-mortem.

Hunter removed his trousers and put them on a hanger, leaving them on the outside of the wardrobe so that he didn't contaminate the fresh clothes inside. He would ask his mum to take his suit to the dry cleaners tomorrow. It was the only way it would get rid of the stench. This was now his second post mortem, and although each of them had been unpleasant viewing, it wasn't the images that remained with him but the fetid stench — a mix of formaldehyde, strong disinfectant and stale blood: the smell of death was not only unique but hung around as an invisible spectre to haunt him.

The autopsy of Derek Vicarage had gone on for almost three hours. Professor Graves had found the bullet lodged in the pulp at the back of Derek's brain. The bullet was .38 and the casing they had found in Derek's bungalow was similar to the ones that had been recovered from Mr Gurmani's shop. It was almost certain now that the people responsible for the robbery had also carried out Derek Vicarage's execution and all for a handful of cash.

He and Barry had returned to the station, but it had been gone 10 pm and the rest of the detectives had gone home. DI Robshaw had still been there and Barry had briefed him on the findings. Robshaw had told them to complete the PM report tomorrow and told them to get off. Barry had wanted to go to the pub but all Hunter wanted was to get out of his stinking clothes, so he made an excuse that he had a splitting headache and caught the bus home.

From downstairs, his mother called, jolting him back to the moment.

'I'm just putting the kettle on, want a cuppa?' she shouted up.

Hunter smiled. What she really wanted was for him to go downstairs and tell her what he had been up to. The robbery and murder would have been on the local news and tomorrow she would be able to give a first-hand report to her friends of what had really happened: she had already told all the neighbours that her son was now in CID. Now, she would be able to elevate his status even further and tell them he was a murder detective.

Following a cup of tea and a cheese sandwich, during which, as he anticipated, he was quizzed by his mum, Hunter retired to his bedroom. He desperately tried to drop off but he couldn't. He read a while, until his eyelids started to droop, then he turned off the light. In the dark he thought about the case. In his mind's eye images of Derek Vicarage's autopsy were playing on a loop.

CHAPTER TWENTY-TWO

Hunter sat at the desk adjoining Barry Newstead's, hammering away at the keyboard of his word processor, finalising the sudden death report of Derek Vicarage. He had got in early to have everything ready for morning briefing. Around him he had been conscious of detectives drifting in, and although he had looked up and acknowledged them, he had not got drawn into their conversation because he wanted to make a good impression and get the paperwork out of the way so that he was available to take on the next set of tasks.

He had just finished reading the report on screen when Barry walked in. As always, he looked his usual untidy self; his thick dark mop of hair had all the appearance of not being brushed and typically his suit was crumpled. Nevertheless, he was still a formidable presence and Hunter knew that his ruffled façade belied his sharp mind.

Barry made for the kettle on top of a cabinet. He picked it up, shook it to check there was enough water in and switched it on. 'Want a cuppa?'

Hunter glanced at his mug. It was half full but the tea was cold. 'Please.'

Barry arranged two mugs. 'I'll make us this and then we'll go down to the report writing room. Briefing's down there this morning. Detectives from District CID are joining us.'

DI Robshaw led the briefing again. For the benefit of the newbies — six detectives from District CID — he retold the story of the robbery and murder before coming to the most recent findings.

'Scenes of Crime tell me that the bullets and casings are similar, and, given that both attacks were committed within hours of one another, I am linking both crimes until evidence tells me otherwise. The stolen vehicle we've recovered from the riverbank is still in the drying room waiting to be examined. I'm told it has taken longer than normal to dry it out because of the weather conditions on the night. However, I am assured that they should be able to begin work on it later this morning.

'With regards to evidence from both crimes, the forensics are going to take at least a week, and the house-to-house at both locations have brought us very little. However, one nugget of evidence came our way last night and it's that I want to focus on today.

'Last night, following the local news report, we got an interesting phone call from the owner of a fish and chip shop, half a mile from The Crescent, who told us about three young men who came into his shop, just after 9.30 on Wednesday night. One of them was covered in blood. When he asked them what they'd been up to they told him they'd been involved in a fight. Luckily for us, he has CCTV installed outside his premises because he's had damage done to both his shop and his car in the past. This is what we've got.'

Robshaw nodded to DS Martin West, who was standing next to a large TV. Martin switched on the TV and then he started the VHS player going. The screen flashed from black to grey, and into view came three young men in Adidas training tops, two of them dressed in joggers and one in jeans, all wearing trainers.

Robshaw nodded his head and Martin paused play. The frozen images of the three men wasn't of good quality — the images had a slight blur — but whereas the images captured on Mr Gurmani's CCTV cameras were of no use whatsoever in assisting with the identification of the robbers, this was of sufficient clarity that anyone who knew any of the individuals would be able to instantly recognise them.

Robshaw said, 'This is on Barnburgh Avenue, as I say, about half a mile away from Derek Vicarage's place, and for those who don't know this area, another half a mile from here this road connects with the country lane where the stolen Ford Fiesta used in the robbery was found crashed.'

Barry craned his head forward. 'Do you know, I think I know who that big git is,' he said. One of the three men on screen was taller and had far wider shoulders than the other two. 'Just run it on a bit, will you?'

Martin set the VHS running again and everyone watched as the three young men walked past the camera, obviously unaware it was there. They were in view for the best part of five seconds before going out of shot.

Robshaw nodded again and the VHS system was paused, freezing the picture on the TV. He said, 'I'll come back to them in a minute, Barry, and you can have another look.' Then addressing the squad, he said, 'It is at this point where they enter the shop. The owner says each of them ordered fish and chips, and the lanky one, as you describe, Barry — by the way he was the one who was covered in blood — took out a wad of notes and paid for the order. The owner says the three of them were laughing and joking while they stood around waiting and then they left. And this is where we pick them up briefly again.'

Robshaw nodded sharply and the VHS was set in play again. Following a few brief flashes of black and white, images of the three young men appeared again. The shot of them was directly beneath the camera and was a lot clearer. The three were conversing with one another, each of them holding a portion of fish and chips in newspaper. The man nearest the camera was cramming fingers full of chips into his mouth.

Martin paused the VHS player once more.

'Well, do you recognise him now, Barry?' asked Robshaw.

'Certainly do,' Barry answered, a huge grin breaking out on his face. 'That's Scott Edwards. The last time he was locked up he was renting a room in a terraced house in Bolton-on-Dearne. He's the guy we think's been responsible for the handbag snatches on the old lasses just lately. I think I recognise the other two as well. I think the one in the middle is Ryan Fisher. If I'm right, Ryan was involved in the handbag muggings with Scott and he's currently on bail. He was picked out on an identification parade by one of the victims whose hip got broken when they knocked her over, but we couldn't get anything on Scott, and Ryan wouldn't grass on him.'

'Well, we've got something on him now,' Robshaw returned.

'The other guy looks a bit like Jordan Stewart,' Barry continued. 'If it is Jordan, I know he's Ryan's mate, but I wouldn't have put Jordan as being mixed up in anything like this. He's a good few years younger than the other two, and if my memory serves me right, he's on probation. He specialises in nicking Ford's for their alloys.'

'Well, let's do some digging, and see if we can confirm or not. I want to make sure we nail all these bastards,' said Robshaw.

It was lunchtime and Hunter had just entered the office with two hot roast pork sandwiches for Barry and himself, when Barry said, 'Don't take your coat off — we'll have to eat those in the car.'

Hunter stopped mid-stride and looked at him.

'We've got to see a man about a dog.'

Hunter threw Barry a puzzled frown. 'A man about a dog?'

'It's a saying, you dumpling. It means we've got to see someone over a bit of business.'

'What bit of business?'

'I'll tell you on route.' Barry dangled a set of car keys. 'I'll take the sarnies, you can drive.' Barry swapped a roast pork sandwich for the set of car keys. Then he took the other sandwich out of Hunter's hand, stepping past him to take the stairs.

In the rear yard of the station, Hunter turned over the engine of the CID car and switched on the screen demister. 'Where're we going?'

'The Rusty Dudley in Goldthorpe,' Barry answered, handing across Hunter's sandwich and biting into his own. 'Someone I haven't seen for years has just rung me to tell me he knows something about the Derek Vicarage shooting and he wants to meet.'

Watching the windscreen slowly clearing, Hunter tore away the top of the paper bag holding his sandwich and took a small bite. In between chewing a mouthful of warm pork and bread, he mumbled, 'Who's it we're going to see?'

'Guy called Mick Woods. I know him from my early days on the beat. I used to bump into him from time to time, either when he'd just finished work, or was on the way to the pub. He used to tell me odd bits of gossip about what was going on in the village, but never gave me information that would actually land anyone in trouble. Mick's a miner, and a big union man, who had a bit of a profile during the strike. Mick's quite a character, as you'll soon see, and to be honest not a fan of the police, especially because of the miner's strike. He sees us as the puppets for the Thatcher Government, so it must be something pretty important if he wants to talk to us.'

'So we're meeting him in the pub?'

'That's where he said he'd be.'

The Rusty Dudley was in the middle of a row of shops on Goldthorpe's high street. There were double yellow lines marking the road so Hunter drove the car onto a side road opposite and parked up.

Barry loosened the knot of his tie, slipped it from his collar and wound it around his hand. 'Take your tie off, lad. Some of the punters in there'll probably know who we are, but we don't want to advertise that we're cops — it's bad for business.'

Hunter removed his tie, pushed it into his coat pocket and got out of the car. It was early afternoon and although the sun was up and the snow had started to melt, it was still bitterly cold. He shuddered as he closed the car door.

Pulling his sheepskin around him, Barry led the way.

The warmth of the pub hit them the moment they entered. The wooden floor was wet and they added to the puddles with the snow they brought in on their shoes. Low-lit, the room was full of drifting smoke and Hunter could hardly make out any of faces now looking their way. He quickly realised why the atmosphere was like this as he scanned the room — it seemed as if just about everyone had a cigarette on the go. A non-smoker himself, it caught in the back of his throat, raising several sharp coughs and he covered his mouth.

Out of the corner of his eye, he caught Barry raise a hand to give a wave of acknowledgment. He looked in the direction his partner was waving, peering through the fug of cigarette smoke to the far corner, where four men were sat around a table. One of the men had his hand in the air. He was thick-set, with short dark hair and looked to be in his thirties. The three men with him rose from their seats, picked up their beers and walked to the opposite side of the room where they took up seats at another table.

'Get three beers,' said Barry and set off across the concert room.

Watching him sauntering away, Hunter shook his head at his partner's cheek; he had already bought the two roast pork sandwiches. Huffing to himself he took out his last tenner, went to the bar and ordered three pints. Clamping the three beers between his hands, watching he didn't spill any, he carefully made his way to where Barry was now sat with the thick-set man. As he shuffled across the floor, he felt vulnerable. It felt as if all eyes were upon him. He could see, however, that Barry didn't look concerned, and taking that as a good sign, he set down the drinks on the table and pulled out a seat opposite.

Barry introduced him. 'This is Hunter. We work together. His dad's the boxing coach at Barnwell Academy. Jock. Do you know him?'

Mick Woods shook his head and held out his hand. He was wearing a t-shirt that was stretched tight over his well-toned chest and arms. Hunter took Mick's hand and shook it. His hand felt coarse, like it had been roughed with sandpaper.

'Nice to meet you, Hunter. I don't know your dad, but I've seen a few of his fighters. I go to all the local boxing dos round here.'

Barry turned to Hunter, slid a beer across to the man and said, 'This is Mick, who I was telling you about. Mick used to work at Barnburgh and Goldthorpe pit.'

'And a lot more, before Thatcher and MacGregor took away our livelihoods,' Mick interjected.

'You can talk to him about anything but don't mention the miner's strike.' Barry let out a short guffaw, put his beer glass to his mouth and sipped the head off his pint.

Mick slapped his hand on the table. 'Don't get me going with that. Bloody Thatcher. That was the biggest injustice this country has ever seen. She destroyed whole communities. If the pits'd been down south that would never have happened. The day she dies, we're going to have one big party round here.'

Hunter noted that Mick had one of the broadest local dialect's he had ever heard.

Barry removed the pint from his mouth and let out another short laugh. 'See what I mean.'

Mick picked the beer up Hunter had bought and took a swallow. Removing the glass, and wiping the froth from his unshaven top lip, he gave a half-smile towards Hunter. 'Barry knows it gets me going.'

'Anyway, Mick, you said you had something to tell me about Derek Vicarage's shooting?' Barry said.

Mick leaned forward and lowered his voice. 'You know I'm no grass, Barry, but there are some things you can't ignore. Derek was one of us. I don't know if you know but Derek used to work at Goldthorpe. He became disabled after getting crushed between tubs. Broke the bottom of his spine and smashed his hips. Put an end to his working days before he was even 30. Derek was a lovely bloke. Never did no harm to anyone. It's shocking what's happened to him and everyone in here wants whoever did this to get what's coming to them.'

'So you know who shot him then?'

'I don't know who exactly shot him, but there's one name floating around as to who's involved.' He paused for a few seconds before saying, 'Jordan Stewart. Do you know him?'

Hunter remembered briefing that morning and what Barry had said. Barry's skills at recollection and recognition of villains were impressive. He hoped within a few years he would be able to match up to him.

Barry nodded.

'Was a nicked Ford Fiesta involved?'

Hunter could feel himself reddening again. Was this ever going away.

Barry nodded again. 'We believe so.'

'Well, the word is that he nicked that, and drove it for two druggy mates of his who did a robbery at a corner shop and that they also did Derek on the same night. Apparently, he's now shitting himself, 'cos he's saying he didn't know that was going to happen.'

'Who's saying all this, Mick?'

Mick returned a smug grin, sat back in his seat, putting his pint glass back to his lips. 'I'm not going to tell you that. The person who told me all this doesn't want to get involved and neither do I. If it wasn't for the fact it was Derek, we wouldn't be having this conversation.' He took a long swallow of his beer.

'I appreciate that, Mick,' Barry replied.

'Good. Now drink up and piss off the pair of you. You're going to give me a bad reputation.'

Barry quickly drained his glass. Scraping back his chair and nudging Hunter, he said, 'We know when we've outstayed our welcome.' Hunter looked up and then at his glass. He still had half his pint left. Barry jerked his head. 'Come on, we need to get back to the nick.' Turning, he glanced back over his shoulder. 'I'll pay you one on as we leave.'

Mick Woods raised his glass. 'My mates'll have one as well. Merry Christmas when it comes.'

CHAPTER TWENTY-THREE

A pale yellow dawn light was breaking between a bank of heavy grey clouds as the raid team, consisting of Hunter and Barry and six firearms officers, turned into the street where Scott Edwards lived. Frosted snow was still in piles at the sides of the road and the van's wheels crunched noisily as it pulled into the kerb, coming to a halt three houses down from the terraced house where Scott Edwards rented the rear downstairs room.

Inside the van, the armed officers went through their final checks while Hunter and Barry watched on. Hunter's heart was racing. The adrenaline had kicked in the moment they had left the station. He looked out through the windscreen. None of the houses showed any signs of life.

The firearms sergeant asked if everyone was ready and following a series of nods shouted, 'Go, go, go!'

The van doors slammed aside and the six officers leaped out, their Heckler & Cock rifles at the ready. Two took the front door and four nipped down the alleyway between the terraced houses, one of them holding the steel battering ram.

Hunter and Barry stepped out of the van onto the icy footpath, listening and looking along the road, waiting for the shout that entry had been gained and the premises secured.

Within two minutes that call came but the nature of the message wasn't what they expected. Hunter and Barry exchanged puzzled looks and made their way to the back yard.

The rear door of the terraced house had been demolished. The top half was hanging off its hinge. Hunter hurried after Barry through a narrow kitchen to the connecting room where one of the officers in black fatigues stood just inside the doorway. His face bore a solemn look.

The room light had been switched on. The décor was red and black. Hunter hurriedly looked around. Everything was so tacky. The first thing that entered his head was that the room reminded him of a brothel.

Scott was tucked up in a single bed pushed against the far wall. Hunter saw that his ashen face was surrounded by a large brown stain. He and Barry edged closer, slipping on gloves. They bent over the bed to get a closer look. Scott was dead and by the paleness of his skin looked to have been dead for some time. He had been shot. A single dark crusted hole had been neatly punched in the centre of his forehead. His left arm was over the top of the quilt and by his hand was a black pistol.

'Suicide?' said Hunter, breaking the silence.

Barry responded with a, 'Hmm.' Straightening, he turned to the firearms officer by the door. 'Did you check if the door was locked before you bashed it in?'

The officer gave Barry a look of disgust. ''Course I checked it. It was definitely locked.'

Barry returned his gaze back to Scott's corpse, leaning in for a closer look at his head. After a few seconds he straightened and turned to Hunter, his mouth set tight. 'I've dealt with a couple of suicides involving firearms before and one of those was with a pistol and it didn't look anything like this. Firstly, there are no burn marks. There should be if he held the gun close to his head. Secondly, there's no blood spatter, and thirdly, since when has anyone ever committed suicide by shooting themselves dead centre in the forehead? They usually shoot themselves just above the ear or put the gun in their mouth or under the chin. Looking at the blood around his head I would say he was lying on his back with his head resting on the pillow when he was shot.' Pointing a finger, Barry continued, 'See, it's just a big pool that's soaked in. And look where the gun is.'

'By his hand.'

'Yes, but which hand?'

'Left hand.'

'And on the CCTV when he robbed Mr Gurmani's shop, which hand was he holding the gun in?'

Hunter thought back to the evidence he had seen. Suddenly he realised what Barry was alluding to. 'Right hand.'

'Exactly. This is not a suicide, matey. Staged to look like one but somebody has shot him.'

Armed officers roused the other three occupants who rented rooms in the terraced house and led them away for questioning. Over the next five hours, Hunter, Barry, and Duncan Wroe from Scenes of Crime, searched the entire property. The only evidence they found was some of the cigarettes and booze from Mr Gurmani's. But there was no cash. Hunter guessed that whoever had killed Scott had taken that.

The pathologist came and went, confirming Barry's observations and arranging to carry out the post-mortem at 6 pm that evening. A couple of the detectives from District, who had been brought in to support the investigation, came from the station to assist with door-to-door enquiries — canvassing for witnesses — and Barry and Hunter borrowed their car so that they could get over to the district custody suite where Scott's partners in crime, Ryan Fisher and Jordan Stewart, were being detained following the other two coordinated early morning raids.

'You believe Ryan or Jordan did this?' Hunter asked, looking across at Barry whose eyes were fixed on the busy road ahead, pushing the car close to the rear of the car in front. He'd already overtaken half a dozen cars, cursing after a couple of the drivers had blared their horns after him.

'Has to be one of them. I can't think of anyone else. Remember the bullet hole in the windscreen of the Fiesta? And the blood?' he answered. He was edging the car into the centre of the road, preparing for another overtake.

Hunter gripped his seat. 'There wasn't that much blood in my car. And the pathologist said Scott had definitely been killed in his bed. Maybe they winged him and then got him back to his house and then topped him there?'

Barry finished his overtaking manoeuvre, shrugging his shoulders as he pulled back to correct side of the road. 'It doesn't make sense at the moment. Let's see what the other two have to say for themselves, shall we?'

Before dealing with Scot's two known co-conspirators, Hunter and Barry interviewed the three residents of the terraced house where Scott's body had been found. After quizzing each of them, it became quite apparent that none of them could assist. Each of them admitted to knowing Scott — more from his reputation than personally — and had steered clear of him. They were all genuinely shocked to learn he had been shot, and when asked if they had heard the sound of gunfire, each of them said that the only thing they had heard last night was loud music coming from Scott's room, which apparently was the norm. To deal with it they merely turned up the sound of their televisions in an attempt to drown out the sound. They all said it was about half past midnight when the music had been finally turned off. All three, much to their relief, were released mid-afternoon after providing statements.

Gathering together those statements, Barry and Hunter grabbed a quick cuppa from the district canteen and then returned to the custody suite. The custody sergeant was really helpful. He told Barry and Hunter that he'd had a few minutes with both of the prisoners when he'd provided them with breakfast a few hours ago, and he told them that Jordan had told him that he was bricking it, and said it was nothing to do with him — it was Ryan.

Barry recalled the conversation with Mick Wood, and he told Hunter that he was going to talk to Jordan first and see what he had to say about the robbery at Mr Gurmani's and the murder of Derek Vicarage, before bringing up Scott's shooting. Barry asked the custody sergeant to contact Jordan's solicitor so that they could interview him, and then he and Hunter retired to the canteen for another cuppa and to plan their interrogation.

Hunter and Barry stepped into the interview room just before noon, taking up the seats opposite Jordan and his solicitor. Jordan threw them a glance and then quickly drew back his gaze, fixing his eyes on the table between them.

As Barry and Hunter made themselves comfortable, the on duty callout solicitor said, 'My client has made a statement to me. He wishes to tell you that he has no knowledge about the death of Scott Edwards and has had no involvement in it whatsoever.'

Barry cleared his throat. 'I'm sure he has, Mr Foster, and Mr Stewart will have his opportunity to have that statement recorded, but before that we have other questions to put to him about a robbery and another murder first.'

Jordan's head shot up. 'That wasn't anything to do with me either,' he proclaimed loudly.

The solicitor reached and touched Jordan's wrist, exchanging glances with him. 'If you feel you cannot answer these detectives' questions, Jordan, then you only have to say that.' The solicitor pulled back his hand and picked up his pen.

Hunter turned on the recording machine, slid in two 45-minute cassette tapes, and went through the preamble and caution prior to interview before asking Jordan if he understood what he had just said.

Jordan nodded.

The solicitor made a note, checking his watch and adding the time.

Barry leaned forward, resting his arms on the table and clenching his fists. His reach was a couple of feet from Jordan — just in striking distance.

Hunter had seen this intimidating tactic many times and smiled inwardly.

Jordan pushed himself back in his chair, fear and nervousness etched in his look.

'Jordan — may I call you Jordan?' Barry didn't wait for an answer. 'Jordan, I first want to talk to you about a robbery at a convenience store on the Tree Estate three days ago.'

'That was nothing to do with me.'

'Well, if it was nothing to do with you can you tell me where you on Tuesday evening?'

'At home.'

'Can anyone verify that?'

'My mum. Ask her, she'll tell you.'

'We have asked her, Jordan. And interestingly she says you were out. She says that your mate Ryan Fisher came to the house about three o'clock and that you didn't get in until gone

10 that night. She also says when you came in you were wet through, and she'd asked you what you'd been up to and you told her you'd got caught in the snow.'

Jordan gulped. 'She must have been mistaken. I think that was Wednesday night she's talking about.'

'Okay, moving on, what do you know about a Ford Fiesta that was stolen from Goldthorpe the night before the robbery I've just mentioned?'

'Nothing.'

Barry hunched a little more forward. 'Well, you see, I'm asking about this Fiesta, because it was used as the getaway car during this robbery, and we found it crashed on the back road to Goldthorpe the morning after the robbery, and it's got some blood on the passenger side and a hole in the windscreen where a bullet went through. I'm mentioning this because a gun was used at the robbery and the owner was shot. Is that jogging any memories?'

'No. I don't know what you're on about.'

'I want you to think about what I've just said, Jordan, because, as we speak, forensics are going over that car very thoroughly. They've collected fibre samples from the seats, and they've collected footprints from the scene where the car was found dumped, and they will be matching those with your clothes and trainers we've seized this morning from your house. You have got form for stealing cars and this one was hot-wired just like the other cars you nicked. If you were inside that car, they will find a match.'

Hunter had been watching Jordan's face during the interview and could see that last question had rattled him. He had visibly paled.

Barry continued, 'We have also found hidden away under your garden shed 26 packets of cigarettes, and nine packets of loose tobacco, all with price stickers from the shop that was robbed.'

Jordan didn't answer.

'What do you have to say about that?'

Jordan looked to his solicitor. 'No comment.'

'As I said a moment ago, the owner of the shop that was robbed, a Mr Gurmani, was shot. Fortunately, he is alive. He was shot in the arm. But it could so easily have proved fatal. This is very serious, Jordan, and I want you to think very carefully about the answers you give.'

'No comment.'

'Jordan, I also mentioned when you first started this interview that I wanted to talk to you about a murder.' He paused and stared across the table. Jordan shied away his eyes. 'An hour after the robbery at Mr Gurmani's shop, a disabled man who lived on The Crescent, at Barnwell, was murdered. He was also shot with the same gun that was used in the robbery. Do you know anything about that?'

'No comment.'

'I'm going to be honest with you here, Jordan, whoever did these crimes is looking at life imprisonment. The innocent man who was shot and killed at The Crescent was no threat to anyone. He was disabled. This is a despicable crime, and if you didn't pull that trigger it would be best if you came clean and told us your involvement, because it's my guess you were merely the getaway driver on both jobs. If that is the case your role was lesser. This is your one and only chance to tell us what happened.'

Jordan was silent for the best part of 30 seconds, then he said, 'Look, this is fuckin' my 'ead in. I didn't have anything to do with those shootings — you've got to believe me.' He paused and met Barry's gaze. 'I'm going to be straight with you now, I did nick the Fiesta. It was Scott and Ryan's idea to do the robbery. Mainly Scott's. They asked me if I'd get them a car and be the driver and they said they'd give me a cut of the money and fags. That was it as far as I was concerned. Nobody said anything about any guns involved. If I'd have known that, I wouldn't have been involved.'

'Do you want to tell us what happened, Jordan?'

Wiping beads of sweat from his top lip and clearing his throat, Jordan answered, 'I nicked the Fiesta just like you said. We nicked another before that, but it was misfiring, so we had a run around and we saw that XR2 parked in a pub car park. I knew it would be a decent set of wheels, so I screwdrivered the lock and then hot-wired it. We dumped the other car at Goldthorpe and then hid the XR2 ready for the job.'

'When you stole the Fiesta did you know it was going to be used in a robbery at that store on the Tree Estate?'

'Yeah, Scott and Ryan told me the week before that they'd been looking at the place and it would be easy. They said they'd been in and bought some booze from there and only the old man was in at night. We went and had a run past it the day after I'd nicked the XR2. Scott said the job would be a doddle.'

'So what happened on Tuesday?'

'It was like you've said, Ryan came round for me and we went round to Scott's and discussed what we were gonna do. Scott had it all planned but I swear I didn't know he had a gun. When we left that evening, he just had those Santa masks as far as I saw. He said it would be a bit of a laugh putting them on. Joked about it being the spirit of Christmas.'

'Did you go straight to the shop?'

'Yeah. When we got there Scott said for me to drive past first. See if anyone was about. We drove past and it was quiet because of the weather. That's when we decided to do it.'

'What happened then?'

'I pulled up outside and Scott and Ryan put the masks on and that's when I saw the gun for the first time. I tell you, I didn't know a shooter was going to be used.'

'Did you say anything?'

'To Scott? No way.' Jordan quickly shook his head. 'He was buzzing. When he's like that you don't say anything. He takes steroids. Makes him pumped up. It's best to keep quiet when he's like that.'

'Did just Scott go in the shop, or Scott and Ryan?'

'Scott and Ryan went. Scott told me to keep the engine running and if anyone was coming, I was to beep the horn three times.'

'And you sat in the car?'

Jordan nodded. 'I tell you, I didn't want to. Seeing Scott with the gun really freaked me out. I just wanted to be out of there. All the time they were in there, I was panicking. And then when I heard the shots, I really freaked out. I didn't know what had gone off.'

'How many shots?'

'I just heard two, and then a couple of minutes later Scott and Ryan came out with carrier bags. They jumped in the car and told me to get them outta there, so I drove as fast as I could.'

'Did you ask what had happened?'

'I didn't need to. Ryan was like me — fuckin' freaked. He was going mental at Scott about him shooting the owner and how he was already on bail. Scott said something about it being an accident — something about the man almost taking his head off with a baseball bat and he hadn't meant to shoot him. I've not seen Ryan like that before. I tell you man, he was really freaked.'

'So where did you go?'

'Scott told me to go up to the woods and park up there for a bit 'cos we knew the feds would be all over the place. I parked behind some bushes so nobody could see us if they came down the lane, though it was snowing by then and hardly anyone was on the roads. Scott lit up this spliff and we shared it and then he counted up the money and the cigs. He was going crazy because he'd only got 170-odd quid. He said he thought there'd be more. Ryan was flapping about the owner being shot. Scott just kept saying it was an accident and that it was the man's own fault — he shouldn't have had a go with the baseball bat. Honest to God, I just wanted to be out of there.'

'What about The Crescent then? The disabled man? How did that come about?'

'That was Scott again. He was going on about he thought there'd be more money and then he just said he knew where he could get more. A lot more than what they'd got from the shop, and that's when he mentioned the disabled guy. "Spas Derek", I think he called him.'

'Did you know who he was on about?'

'No, I've never heard of him. Ryan did though. As soon as Scott mentioned him Ryan freaked out again. Scott said he had pots of money in his house and that Ryan had got no bottle. That's when he said we should go there and rob him.'

'What about you. Did you say anything?'

Jordan shook his head vigorously. 'No fucking way. I tell you Scott was on one. I was fucking scared he'd shoot me. I kept my trap shut. Scott just said we were doing it and that was that. He told me where to drive.'

'To The Crescent?'

Jordan nodded. Sweat had now formed in his hairline. 'It was really snowing by then. The roads were well dodgy but there was no one about and Scott showed me where to go. Scott pointed out his house and told me to park just down the road.'

'Who went into the house?'

'It was a bungalow. Scott and Ryan went. Scott told him to put on the masks 'cos he thought Derek would recognise him.'

'And you stayed in the car?'

'Yeah, same as before. I was to beep the horn again if they needed warning.'

'And then what happened?'

'They were in the house a good ten minutes and then they came running out and told me to drive. Scott was waving a load of cash. Couple of grand I think.'

'Was anything said about anyone being shot?'

'You mean Derek?'

'Yes.'

'Not then. We'd gone down the road, and Scott just said he was starving and that there was a chippy near where we were. He told me to pull in and made a joke about tea being on him and flashed the cash. We went to the chippy and Scott got fish and chips for us all, and that's when the guy who was serving asked Scott how he'd got the blood on him. That's when I saw the blood on his trackie top. There were splashes down the front and I think there was some on his arm. He told the guy he'd been in a fight.'

'Is that when you learned Derek had been shot?'

'Not in the chippy. No.'

'I didn't mean him telling you in the chippy.'

'Oh sorry, yeah, when we came out. I asked Scott what had gone off and it was Ryan who said that Scott had shot Derek. Scott was well fucked off with him, saying it was his fault — he should have kept his mouth shut. I didn't know what they were on about and I didn't want to ask because Scott was getting really revved up by then.

'Ryan said he felt sick and spewed his guts up. Scott told him he'd better pull himself together. Then he told me to take him home and dump the car. He was really fucked off with Ryan. When we got on the back lane Scott started having a go at him, saying it was all his fault, and how if he hadn't have mentioned his name, Derek would still be alive. When I heard that, I almost spewed up missen. Ryan started shouting about us getting done for murder, and then Scott started waving the gun at Ryan, telling him he'd shoot him if he didn't shut the fuck up.

'They were going at one another. Scott started waving the gun in his face and Ryan grabbed it. There was a bit of a struggle and the gun went off and that's when I crashed the car. The car skidded and went through the hedge and we ended up down by the river. It was a good job those rocks were there otherwise we would have ended up in it. I tell you, I have never been so fucking scared in all my life. I just wanted to be out of there.'

'Who got shot then? We found the bullet hole in the windscreen and the blood. Was it Scott?'

'The bullet nicked the top of his ear when him and Ryan were having a go at one another. He was dead lucky, you know. It could have killed him.'

Barry's face took on a probing look. 'So Scott wasn't seriously hurt then?'

'No, but he was fucking shocked, I tell you. Then he got fucking annoyed when he realised his ear was bleeding. It had taken a chunk out of it. The cops who locked me up said Scott had been found dead in his bed. Is that right?'

Barry nodded. 'We found Scott dead in his bed this morning. He'd been shot in the head.'

'Well, that was definitely nowt to do with me. I swear down.'

'Jordan, when you were brought in you said to the custody sergeant who booked you in that you needed to speak with Ryan. Why did you say that?'

'Because when I left Scott, he was still alive. I've got witnesses.'

'Just hold it there, Jordan. Tell me what happened after the gun went off in the car, when Scott and Ryan were fighting.'

'It was as I was saying. Scott was waving the gun, Ryan grabbed it and it just went off. I went into a total panic. We skidded off the road and went through the hedge and ended up almost going in the river. Like I say, those rocks stopped us. Scott started going mental when he felt his ear bleeding, started shouting it was all Ryan's fault. The gun must have got knocked out of his hand when we crashed and he started looking around for it. I think Ryan thought Scott was going to shoot him and so he jumped out of the back and legged it. He was up the banking and gone, leaving me with Scott. It took me ages to calm him down. He said he was going to kill Ryan.'

'What happened then?'

'He told me to wipe the car down, while he tried to stop his ear bleeding. I used my t-shirt and wiped the steering an' all that. Then Scott said we'd best go to his place and he'd sort the cash from Derek's — give me my cut. I told him I didn't want any. We went over the fields and when we came out at the back of the estate, we saw Chloe, that mad Goth bird of his. I think he dumped her a few weeks ago but she wouldn't take no, 'cos she's a psycho. She had this bottle of cider and said she was just on her way up to his place. Scott said to me, "Well, this is my shag sorted for the night", low-like, so she couldn't hear and he went off with her. I was so glad, I tell you. He was so revved up I didn't want to be with him.'

'So you went home then?'

'Yes. I got in just after 10. My mum's already told you.'

'And you didn't have any of the money from Derek's?'

'No, Scott hadn't sorted it and I didn't want any. He just gave me the fags and my split from the shop. That's the stuff you found under our shed.'

'And what about Ryan?'

Jordan shrugged his shoulders. 'First I've seen him since the robbery was this morning when we were locked up.'

'And Scott?'

'Same. I've kept away from him. I saw it all on the news. I've been shitting myself. I swear, I didn't know they'd killed Derek until Ryan had a go at Scott in the car.'

'And you're saying that the last you saw of Scott was when you left him on his street on the night Derek was killed?'

'Yeah, check with his ex, Chloe. She's my witness. As far as I know she was going back to his house. I left them and haven't seen Scott since. I've stayed well away from the pair of them since it happened. I've been crapping myself. When you lot first came this morning, I thought it was about the robbery and Scott shooting Derek. When those two detectives told me Scott had been shot as well, I thought they were joking.' Jordan paused, grabbing a lung full of air. 'I'm telling you, don't pin this on me. You need to be having a word with Ryan, if anyone.'

Hunter and Barry went back over Jordan's answers with him, but except for elaborating on some elements of his story, he didn't deviate from the main crux of his confession and after a short meeting with his solicitor he was placed back in his cell.

Following a snack of a sandwich and bag of crisps, the pair updated DI Robshaw over the phone, and returned to the cell area to speak with Ryan.

They had expected a difficult interview, given his greater involvement than Jordan, and especially with his solicitor advising him beforehand, but except for some initial hesitancy, the moment Ryan was faced with Jordan's testimony, and the CCTV evidence from Mr. Gurmani's, he opened up.

Ryan was visibly shaking as he started his confession, immediately blaming Scott for both shootings and, just like Jordan, he pointed out that he hadn't known Scott was armed until they pulled up outside the convenience store and he produced the handgun as they were about to get out of the car.

With prompting from Barry, Ryan gave a detailed account of what had happened inside the corner shop, which mirrored that of Mr Gurmani's statement. Happy with that, Barry quizzed him as to what had happened at Derek Vicarage's place. Once again, Ryan was forthcoming, completely laying the blame at Scott's feet as to whose idea it was to rob Derek, explaining in detail what had gone on inside his bungalow and how Scott had threatened Derek, hit him with the gun across the face, cutting his cheek, and then pressing the barrel of the gun against his forehead until he'd told them where he had his money hidden.

Ryan admitted it was he who had found the stash underneath Derek's mattress and he had also found some money in a tin inside his wardrobe. He said he hadn't counted it but he thought there must have been at least 2000 pounds.

When the interview came to the point of Derek's killing, Ryan was silent for the best part of a minute, looking to his solicitor as if he was going to provide him with the answer, but just as Barry had been about to prompt him, he turned, looked at both Barry and Hunter and replied, 'All I did was call Scott's name. It was by accident, I wasn't thinking. Derek said he wasn't going to say anything. He said we could take his cash but Scott just shot him.'

'Just shot him?' said Barry.

'Yeah. In the head. I couldn't believe it. I mean the bastard in the shop had had a go at Scott with the bat, that's why he was shot, but this was different.'

'You mean Derek Vicarage was an invalid and couldn't do anything like that?'

Ryan flushed. 'I never wanted this to happen. I swear. It was Scott. He's mental.'

'*Was* mental. Remember, he's dead. He was shot. We found his body this morning.'

'That's what the detectives told me when they arrested me. Who shot him?'

'That's what I'd like to ask you.'

Ryan's mouth dropped open. His face took on a look of shock. 'You don't think it was me, do you?'

'Well, we know you and he had a fight in the car back from Derek's place, and we know the gun was discharged and Scott got the top of his ear shot off.'

'Whoa, fuck me! That was an accident. Totally fucking accidental. Scott was waving the gun in my face. I thought he was going to shoot me because I was blaming him for killing Derek. I grabbed it and it went off. When I saw it had taken the top off his ear, I fucking legged it home. I thought he'd shoot me if he got the chance, he was so wound up. I haven't seen him since. I've kept my head down. I told my mum if Scott came round to tell him I wasn't in. She doesn't like him anyway. She blames him for me getting done for nicking those handbags from those old lasses.'

'So you're saying that after you left Scott and Ryan, you legged it home and you haven't been near his house or seen Scott since?'

'No way. I'm being fucking straight with you. I had nothing to do with Scott getting shot. Have you spoken with Jordan? I left those two together when I legged it.'

The evening briefing focussed on Barry and Hunter's interview with Jordan and Ryan and the post-mortem of Scott. The autopsy revealed that Scott had been killed during a two-hour window between 10 pm and midnight the previous day. That timing roughly coincided with the residents' statements of music being played loudly until about 12.30 am.

The pathologist found that Scott had lost a small portion of his right ear, as a result of the handgun being discharged during his struggle with Ryan, and as had been surmised from the professor's earlier examination at Scott's home, Scott had indeed been laid flat on his bed, with his head resting on the pillow, when he had been shot.

The bullet had been found in the mush of his brain and the trajectory of the shot showed that whoever had executed him had been standing above him, the gun barrel several feet from his forehead when the trigger had been pulled. The mystery was who that person was. Both Jordan and Ryan had denied it, and a check on their alibi's — that they were at home — so far, stood up to scrutiny.

Before calling it a day, Robshaw made it a point that the team should work on their defence tomorrow, as well as clarify the identity of Scott's ex-girlfriend Chloe. She was the one independent witness who would be able to confirm Jordan's story that he had walked away from Scott at least an hour before he was murdered.

CHAPTER TWENTY-FOUR

Hunter had another restless night, tossing and turning in his bed, his head so full of slop from the past few days, that he finally gave up on sleep just after 6 am, rolled out of bed, showered and made his way on foot into work. He had expected to be first in, and so was surprised when he saw Barry at his desk, his big hands encasing a mug of tea.

Barry looked up as Hunter entered, a grin breaking across his mouth. 'Got to you as well, eh?'

Hunter shucked off his coat and draped it over his chair. 'I've been mulling over who might have shot Scott and thinking have we missed something. I couldn't sleep.' He set down his briefcase on his desk, went across to the kettle, switched it on and grabbed a mug, placing a teabag inside.

'Well, we've got some work to do on Jordan and Ryan's alibi's this morning and we've got this Chloe girl to talk to. Then we'll have another crack at the pair and see if a night in the cells has done anything to change their story.'

Hunter had just poured boiling water over his teabag when the office door opened. He looked over his shoulder to see Sergeant Marrison standing in the doorway.

'Morning, Bob,' Barry greeted. 'To what do we owe this pleasure?'

'Morning, Serge.' Hunter dared not call him by his first name. It was unwritten protocol for someone of his short service. He would always be 'Serge', unless Hunter got invited to call him by his first name or until he himself got promoted to the same rank.

'The lads told me you two were in early. I've got something that you might be interested in.'

'What's that then, Bob?' Barry responded, putting down his mug.

'Roger has just radioed in from the hospital. He turned out to an ambulance call half an hour ago — a young lass had taken an overdose — looks like a serious attempt. The mother told Roger that she's found a load of money in her room and doesn't know where it's from and that her daughter was going on about doing something awful.'

Hunter whipped his eyes away from Sergeant Marrison and met his partner's gaze. Barry's face bore a look of excitement.

'I thought that would grab your interest.' Sergeant Marrison tore the top sheet of paper from his pad and slapped it down in front of Barry. 'That's her details and address. Roger is with her now at the hospital. I've just spoken to him and he says she's been treated by the doctor but she'll be staying for a good few hours at least.'

Picking the note up, Barry pushed back his chair and waved it in Hunter's direction. 'No time for tea, matey, I think our puzzle as to who shot Scott might have just been solved.'

At the hospital reception, Hunter and Barry were directed to A & E. They entered a treatment area already bustling with activity at the early hour of 8.30 am. Barry stopped in front of a nurse carrying a bundle of X-Rays. He enquired after Chloe Winterman — the name on the sheet of paper Sergeant Marrison had handed him. She pointed them to a curtained cubicle at the end of a line of bays and they headed towards it.

At the cubicle, Barry stopped and listened for a couple of seconds. Then he whipped aside the curtain. A quartet of heads turned their way. One of those was Roger, who had been told to keep watch over Chloe. He registered their arrival with a nod. The other three people in the cubicle were Chloe and a man and woman in their 40s who Hunter guessed were her parents.

The first thing Hunter noted about Chloe was her shock of jet-black hair interlaced with streaks of electric blue. Her eyes were rimmed with thick black liner, some of which had run onto her cheeks. She was lying in a trolley bed, half propped against a bank of pillows. Chloe's parents locked onto his gaze and he issued a comforting smile.

Roger stepped out of the bay without saying a word, letting the curtain close behind him.

Drawing him a few yards from the cubicle, Barry said to Roger on a low note, 'Your sergeant said that her parents found her being sick this morning and she'd told them she'd taken an overdose.'

Roger nodded. 'Apparently it was her dad who heard her being sick. She told him straight away that she'd taken a load of paracetamol and so they called for an ambulance. Before it got there, her dad made her drink saltwater, which made her throw up even more. She's been seen by a doctor who's waiting for the blood results and he's referred her to the on call psychiatrist. It would appear she'd already undergone a psychiatric assessment a few years ago after she attacked her teacher and did a similar thing.'

Barry raised his eyebrows thoughtfully. Then he said, 'Sergeant Marrison said that her mum told you that she said she'd done something awful and that she's found a load of cash in her bedroom.'

Roger again nodded. 'I haven't spoken with Chloe because the sergeant told me that you were on your way, but yes, her mum did tell me that before the ambulance arrived Chloe was going on about "doing something awful" and that she was "sorry". Chloe hasn't said much else and I haven't spoken with her because of your enquiry. To be honest, I haven't had any time to chat with her. The doctor's not long finished dealing with her.'

'Good.' Barry tapped his shoulder. 'And the money? What did her mum say about that?'

'The ambulance was still at the house when I got there. The paramedics were just bringing Chloe downstairs. Her mum took me up to her bedroom and showed me the money. There was a wad of notes on her dressing table. Fives, tens and twenties. I didn't have time to count it but it looks at least a couple of grand. I've left it there and told her mum to leave it where it was and we'd sort it later. We all came straight here. Her parents came in the ambulance with her and I followed in the car.'

'Okay. Has the doctor said anything about Chloe being well enough to talk to?'

'I did ask the doctor who saw to her if we were okay to ask her questions, and he said she was fine to talk, if she wants to, and her parents are okay with that. They need to keep her in until she's seen the psychiatrist and they've got her blood results back.'

Barry diverted his eyes, setting them on Hunter. 'Are you good to go then, partner? Let's see if we can clear our mystery up.'

Before Hunter had time to nod, Barry was pulling open the cubicle curtain.

Chloe Winterman looked their way as Barry and Hunter entered. Barry was wearing a big friendly smile. 'Good morning,' he said cheerfully. Setting his eyes on Chloe, he continued, 'You had everyone scared there for a moment,

Chloe — now what was all that about?' Before she had time to answer he switched his gaze to her parents, 'Am I all right to ask your daughter a few questions, Mr and Mrs Winterman?'

Hunter watched Chloe's mum and dad look at one another, then at their daughter. Chloe shied away her eyes.

Mrs Winterman took her hand and gave it a squeeze.

Mr Winterman said, 'Is she in any trouble?'

Barry plonked himself down at the bottom of her bed. 'I'll be perfectly honest with you, we think she's got mixed up with a wrong 'un. Does the name Scott Edwards mean anything to you?'

'Is that the Scott you've been going out with, Chloe?' Mrs Winterman asked her daughter.

Chloe's gaze was fastened firmly on the sheets covering her. She never looked up but nodded in response to the question.

Barry asked, 'Do you know why we're here, Chloe?'

'I can guess.'

'It's about Scott.'

Chloe's mouth set tight.

'We've currently got two lads locked up for robbery and murder. One of them is called Jordan Stewart. Do you know Jordan?'

She gave a sharp nod. 'I know him vaguely. I know he's one of Scott's mates. I've seen them knocking around together a couple of times.'

'Well, he knows you, and he says that the night before last, around 9.30, he saw you on Scott's street holding a bottle of cider, and that Scott told him you and he were off to the house where Scott lives. Is that correct?'

She again nodded.

'Did you go straight to Scott's house?'

'Yes.'

'What did you do there?'

'We shared the cider I'd bought and Scott had some cans of strong lager afterwards. Two cans, I think. I didn't want any. Then we watched a bit of telly.'

'Anything else?'

She didn't answer. Instead she looked to her mother.

'How do you know Scott, Chloe?'

She pulled back her gaze. 'We used to go out.'

'He was your boyfriend?'

'Yes.'

'How long for?'

'Five, six months.'

'When did you break up?'

'A couple of weeks ago.'

'But you're still friends?'

'Sort of.'

'What do you mean, sort of?'

She again looked to her mother. Her face was tinged with sadness and regret. She said softly, 'I'm sorry, Mum.'

Mrs Winterman's face took on a look of concern.

'Do you want to tell us what happened to Scott, Chloe?'

Her eyes still firmly engaged with her mum, she said, 'I'm really sorry, Mum, I didn't mean it. It just happened.'

Mrs Winterman's hand leapt to her mouth. 'Oh my God.'

'It was an accident.'

Barry asked, 'How did you kill him, Chloe?'

She brought back her eyes and set them on Barry. 'His gun went off by accident.'

Mrs Winterman let out a cry. 'Oh my God, Chloe!'

Barry diverted his gaze for a split-second and then returned to Chloe. 'While he was in bed?'

She nodded.

'Do you want to tell us about it, Chloe?'

'It was because of Sally Clayton.'

'What do you mean, it was because of Sally Clayton? Who's Sally Clayton?'

'She's someone I know from the pub. She's always throwing herself at Scott every time we go there and I found out a couple of weeks ago he'd been with her behind my back. And he'd told everyone about it. I asked him why, and he said because she was a better shag than me.'

'Did you have a row with Scott last night about that, Chloe?'

She nodded sharply. 'He was laughing at me. He'd told all my mates. I saw the gun on the side, and I don't know why but I picked it up and told him to stop laughing at me. Instead he laughed even more and told me I should get a life. I was so angry. I just meant to frighten him. I didn't mean to kill him. I thought the gun was just a toy and I pulled the trigger.'

In the George and Dragon, Barry set down a pint in front of Hunter and took his seat opposite. Barry took a large swallow of beer, wiped the froth from his bushy moustache and let out a contented sigh.

Hunter looked across at his partner. 'Quite a day, Barry.'

'You're telling me. It's a long time since I've put in these kind of hours. Good result, though.'

'Quite sad though about Chloe, don't you think?'

'What is?'

'She's going to get charged with murder.'

'Don't you start getting all sentimental, young Hunter. One of the first rules in being a detective is you don't do sentimental. No matter what that shit hole said to her, she had a choice. That gun was on the bedside cabinet. She had to think about picking it up, aim it and pull the trigger. And, anyway, you heard what she said about thinking it was a toy. She's not going to get charged with murder. It's more than likely going to be manslaughter. In a few years she'll be out.

'And another thing. Chloe wasn't that innocent. You heard what the doctor said about her medical condition. That young lady has been undergoing cognitive behaviour therapy for her anger. Five years ago she attacked one of her teachers with a pair of scissors because she excluded her for bullying another pupil. She was lucky not to go to prison for that.

'That girl has got issues, Hunter. Thankfully, it was Scott who crossed her this time and not someone innocent.' He paused, grabbing another large swallow of beer before continuing. 'I tell you what is sad. That Scott didn't get to spend the next 20 years in prison, probably even longer, given what he did to Derek Vicarage.' He took another large swallow of his pint, emptying the glass. Wiping his moustache, he said, 'Do you want another before we hit the road? I'm only having a swift one. We've got a busy day tomorrow. We've got all the charges to prepare and three remand files to knock up.'

Hunter glanced at his pint. He still had half of it left. He replied, 'No thanks, Barry. To be honest, I'm absolutely knackered. I haven't slept for three days with what's been going on and I'm ready for my bed.'

Barry pushed himself up. 'Lightweight,' he laughed. 'You know you'll have to get more stamina if you want CID? There'll be many days like this one when you get in.'

Hunter eyed him thoughtfully. 'Do you think I've got a chance of getting in, Barry?'

'Every, from what I've seen. You've certainly got a nose for detecting crime. Like I said before, you've put some detectives to shame these last few weeks. The DI's already taken notice.

Get your probation in, keep doing what you're doing and I can see you knocking on the door in another couple of years.'

As Barry turned and aimed for the bar, Hunter felt his mood lifting.

Hunter strolled the mile home in a peaceful frame of mind. He felt weary from sleep deprivation, and yet at the same time was in a buoyant mood. Barry's words were swilling around inside his head and he replayed them constantly as he walked. *The DI's taken notice.* Now, he had to just keep up the momentum. Every opportunity there was to get involved in detecting crime, grasp it.

As he rounded the corner of his street, he could see his home was in darkness. His parents had retired to bed. He was ready himself. He tiptoed down the drive to the front door and inserted the key in the lock as quietly as he could. He could sleep for a fortnight but knew he had to set the alarm for 6.30 am ready for the off. It would be another busy day tomorrow.

CHAPTER TWENTY-FIVE

It was a crisp, clear morning, and the sharp chill was what Hunter needed to refresh himself as he walked into work. The half hour it took to get to the station gave him some thinking time to sort out what his immediate priorities were once he got in. Before going upstairs, he checked his tray to ensure there was no pressing enquiries that needed responding to and, satisfied there wasn't, he made his way to the CID office. He was the first in, and checking his watch, knowing that Barry wouldn't be too far behind him, he filled up the kettle and switched it on.

The kettle had only just boiled when Barry appeared, shucking off his sheepskin coat and throwing it across the nearest desk.

Hunter lined up two mugs with teabags and mashed them both a brew, handing one to Barry.

Barry held it between his big hands, blowing the surface. 'Just what I need, this, before we make a start. Busy day ahead with paperwork today, I'm afraid. I'll show you how to knock the charges together for those three in the cells, once we get the final decision from CPS, and then I'll show you how to put a remand file together. All good experience this, Hunter,' he finished, taking a swallow of hot tea.

Barry set the mug down on his desk and picked out several pieces of paper from his tray — notes from the previous day's action and interview. He had a good fistful.

'Right, I'll put these into some sort of order so they make sense and we'll make a start on our evidence.'

For the next hour and a half, Barry and Hunter sat side by side writing evidence into their pocket books dictated by Barry. Hunter had to shake his hands several times to release cramp. It was the longest chain of testimony he had written since joining. On several occasions they were disturbed by detectives involved in the hunt for Dylan Wolfe sticking their head through the door, bidding them good morning, making a brief congratulatory comment about their job yesterday before disappearing again. Hunter's emotions were running at an all-time high. He could never have imagined he would have been involved in something as high profile as this so early in his career and he didn't want this attachment to end.

The pair had just finished writing up their pocket books when a phone rang on the next desk and a male voice shouted from the other side of the office door, 'That's a call for PC Kerr. The caller was put through to the incident room by mistake. I don't know who it is and he won't give his name.'

Throwing Barry a puzzled look, Hunter rose, shouted 'Got it,' and picked up the handset. 'PC Kerr,' he announced.

A muffled but discernible voice said, 'It's Jud. Jud Hudson. I promised I'd give you a call. You still looking for Dylan Wolfe?'

Hunter felt his heart leap. He transferred the handset to his other ear and snatched up a pen and a scrap of paper from the table. 'Do you know something, Jud?'

'Nobody must know I gave you this. Are we clear?' the faint voice continued.

The voice was so stifled that Hunter had a mental picture of Jud covering the mouthpiece with a hand. He replied, 'Absolutely.'

'And then you and I are straight?'

'We are, Jud.'

'No comebacks?'

'No comebacks, Jud.'

'Good, take this down then.' Jud rattled off the location where Dylan Wolfe was and upon finishing, hung up without a goodbye.

Hunter snatched up his note, meeting Barry's gaze.

Barry said, 'That's a face that tells me you've got something. And I gather from that conversation it's come from Jud Hudson?'

Hunter nodded. 'He's only gone and told me where he believes Dylan Wolfe is hiding.'

'Come on then, don't keep me in suspenders. Spit it out.'

Hunter let out a laugh. 'He says Dylan's down on the old Manvers Coking Plant site.'

Barry's brow tightened. 'Anywhere specific? That's a big area.'

'It is, but Jud says he's been holed up in one of the offices for these past few days. He's just taken delivery of a vehicle — a Nissan Bluebird — red — from Big Baz who owns the breakers yard at Kilnhurst and he's got a place lined up somewhere in London to keep his head down. Somebody Baz knows.'

'That shit's involved, is he?' Barry thrust himself out of his chair and snapped up a bunch of car keys. 'The old coking plant it is then. Come on, we'll go in the CID car and see if we can catch ourselves a big fish.'

Hunter launched himself up. 'What about back-up?'

Barry balled his big right hand into a fist and held it up. 'This is all the back-up we'll need. Besides, we don't know if he's still there or not. He might have already done a runner. We'll call for back-up if something materialises.'

Inside a quarter of an hour, Barry was pulling the CID car off the main road and onto a narrow dirt track which led towards the old coking plant. Overgrown hedges flanked either side of the potholed track, scraping the sides of their unmarked Peugeot as it bumped and rocked across ruts of icy mud and compacted coal dust. A hundred metres in, the track opened up to a wider trail, with ditches either side. At the end of it was a pair of battered, half open, metal gates, an old security sign hanging at an angle upon them.

Barry slowly edged forward in the CID car, the engine only giving out low revs. Hunter's eyes scoped everywhere, looking for movement, or a trace of the red Nissan that Jud had passed him, but all he saw was the high black sides of the derelict coking plant that stretched for several hundred metres. 50 metres inside the compound, Barry turned off the engine, coasting for a short distance before coming to a halt.

They both wound down their windows and listened. The place was eerily silent. Not even the sound of bird life could be heard.

Hunter was just doing a second sweep when Barry hissed, 'Over there.'

Hunter whipped his gaze sideways to where Barry's outstretched arm was pointing beyond the driver's side window. He followed the line to where, 200 metres ahead, he could just make out a red car roof appearing above a line of old rusting coal tubs.

'You did say it was a red Bluebird?' said Barry.

Hunter nodded. 'That's what Jud said.'

'That red roofs good enough for me. Shall we see if our friend is with it then?'

Barry started up the car again and inched the Peugeot forward towards the old coal tubs idling on red rusted rails.

100 metres from their quarry, Barry brought the CID car to a standstill. He nudged Hunter and whispered, 'Just check it out. If he's in the car give me a shout.'

Hunter hardly made a sound as he opened the car door. Checking his footing, avoiding a frozen puddle, he straightened his coat and zeroed in on his target. Hunching down into a crouch, he set off at a trot towards the coal wagons. Poking his head around the wagon he had a view of the rear and offside of the Nissan. He made out that someone was in the front seat, head set back against the headrest, as if in slumber. Hunter looked back at his partner and gave the thumbs up, and then, stepping up onto the balls of his feet, ready for a sprint, he sneaked out from behind the coal tubs.

Hunter saw that the driver's side window was half down. The driver was still in recumbent position. Taking a deep breath, he dashed forward and grabbed at the door handle, giving it a yank. But the door didn't open. The locks were down and Hunter lost his grip. Dylan Wolfe was awake in a flash and reaching for the dashboard.

In an instant Hunter realised why. A knife was parked just above the steering wheel.

Dylan snatched it up and thrust it towards Hunter.

The blade shot through the half open window and, thanks to his swift footwork, missed Hunter by a few inches. His yelled back over his shoulder, 'Barry, he's got a knife.' Instinctively, moving into boxing stance, he swallowed the lump in his throat and said, 'Just calm down, Dylan. There's no need for this.'

'You're not fucking taking me in,' Dylan shouted, waving the menacing blade at Hunter.

Hunter dropped his arms but kept his fists clenched. 'Come on, don't be stupid, Dylan, this is only gonna make things worse.'

'Back off. NOW!'

Hunter's brain was whirling. He locked onto Dylan's cold-blooded glare. Licking dry lips, he said, 'Come on, be sensible. We can get this sorted out. Kim's gonna be all right. Just give me the knife and we can forget this ever happened.' He offered his right hand, palm open.

'Fuck off with the bullshit.'

'I'm not bullshitting, Dylan. Give me the knife and I'll say you came quietly.'

Hunter saw Dylan's face change. The hard granite stare became a blank look. Hunter took a step nearer.

In that instant Dylan catapulted himself forwards and with a whiplash movement threw out his arm. The knife he'd been clutching whizzed through the gap in the driver's window.

Hunter tried to react but he had hardly turned before the blade hit him in the chest. Automatically, he staggered back and let out a gasp.

'You're fucking lying,' Dylan screamed and fired up the Bluebird's engine.

Clawing at his chest, Hunter felt the knife brush the front of his top coat as it fell towards the floor. His eyes snapped down to where the blade had hit and he heaved out a huge sigh as he realised it had struck his radio in his inside breast pocket. He snatched up his eyes again at the sound of grit and gravel being churned up. The Bluebird's wheels were spinning in icy mush as it lurched forward, tearing away.

For a split-second Hunter had to catch himself, his legs momentarily turning to jelly, but then his thoughts were back to the moment and he became conscious of the CID car speeding towards him. The passenger door swung open as it slowed alongside and Hunter leapt into the front seat, scrambling around for the seatbelt. In front, through a veil of slushy coal dust and dirt he could make out Dylan's getaway car snaking haphazardly towards the exit gates.

He snatched up the car radio to broadcast their pursuit. But before he had even begun to speak, he saw the red car swerving violently. For a second, he watched it slide sideways and then the rear end started to buck. Hunter could hear the Nissan's engine scream as an uncontrollable spin followed. Seconds later, it smashed into the metal gates, sending fragments of rusting steel every which way, as it careered through the gap and impacted into a grass bank. There was an almighty thump as the Bluebird bounced upwards, spun 180 degrees in the air before coming back to land on its roof with a sickening crunch.

The CID slewed to a halt yards from the crash and before Barry had even applied the handbrake Hunter was throwing open the passenger door and scrambling from his seat.

As Hunter approached the upturned Nissan, he could hear Dylan screaming. The upside-down car was steaming. The roof was crumpled and Hunter had to drop to his knees to see inside. Dylan Wolfe was hanging upside down, his neck at an awkward angle as his head pressed against the inside of the roof. His legs were trapped inside a squashed bulkhead. Hunter's eyes were everywhere as his thoughts clawed at prioritising what needed to be done. The situation looked perilous and Dylan's face was ghostly white.

'Get me out!' he screamed. 'Get me fucking out of here!'

Hunter sank even further, and on all fours, he crawled part way inside the car. He put his hands around Dylan's neck in an attempt to support his head but his bodyweight was too great. Dylan continued to scream and the pitch hurt Hunter's ears.

Hunter saw that Dylan's right eye was beginning to swell and he was bleeding from his mouth. As he screamed, the blood bubbled and foamed.

Hunter said, 'Try and keep calm! The ambulance and fire brigade are on their way. We'll soon have you out.'

Dylan stopped screaming and began whimpering, 'I can't feel my legs.' He reached out and grabbed Hunter's wrist. 'I'm going to die, aren't I?'

'No, you're not. We'll have you out of here in no time. Just hold on, it won't be long.' Hunter could feel through his grip that Dylan's was beginning to tremble. He continued to support his head and hold his gaze. It was then that he noticed that Dylan's pupils were starting to dilate. Hunter knew it was not a good sign. He gently moved his head. 'Come on, Dylan, hang in there. It's not going to be long now.'

Dylan's breathing became shallower. He started to mumble, 'I'm dying, aren't I?'

Hunter knew things were not good and he knew he needed to say something comforting. He replied, 'No, you're not, Dylan.'

'I am! I know I am.' Dylan gasped and drew in a deep breath. 'I don't want to die.'

'It's okay. We're going to get you out. Just hang on in there.'

Tears began forming in the corner of Dylan's eyes and closing them, he said softly, 'I did June, you know. I didn't mean for her to die. She recognised me from the club.'

'I know. You don't need to talk about it right now. Just concentrate on getting out of here.'

Dylan took a deep breath. His chest wavered. 'I'm sorry, about the other women as well.' He let out a prolonged sigh and then his body went limp.

In the distance the sound of sirens were getting louder.

CHAPTER TWENTY-SIX

Barry took another long slug of his beer. When he removed it from his mouth less than a quarter of the pint was left. He looked at it and then at Hunter. 'Fancy another?'

Hunter was only half way down his. He shook his head. 'No, this is my third. I can't drink anymore. I'm finishing this and then going home. It's been a long week. I'm knackered.'

Barry supped the last dregs of his beer and pushed himself up. 'Lightweight.' In his large hand he pointed his empty glass at Hunter. 'We're going to have to build you up, you know. It's the statutory requirement of a detective to get pissed when a job comes together. Look at that lot.' Barry pointed back to the bar which was rammed three-deep with detectives. The murder team, as well the rape enquiry team had overtaken the bar and were celebrating in style.

Dylan Wolfe's confession to Hunter had sealed his fate, plus, when they had seized his clothing, they had found him wearing a pair of woman's pants that they believed belonged to Elizabeth Barnett and they were anticipating that when the DNA results came back, they would fully support that admission.

Dylan Wolfe was in hospital. The Fire Service had to cut apart the vehicle to get him out and then he had been transported by ambulance. He had suffered a fractured sternum and four busted ribs, and had also smashed the tibia and fibula of his right leg, but he had survived the crash. A few weeks in hospital and then he would be remanded to prison to await trial. He was looking at a long time behind bars.

Barry pushed himself up, laying a hand on Hunter's shoulder as he passed. 'I'll tell you one thing, Hunter, you're not just the DI's blue-eyed boy, but the detective superintendent's as well. You've saved him thousands on his budget. You keep your nose clean for the next two years and you'll definitely be in CID.' He let out a loud guffaw and made his way to the bar.

Fastening his overcoat, Hunter stood a moment at the pub entrance looking out along the High Street. Shop fronts were aglow with fairy lights and festooned with everything Christmas. It jogged Hunter's thoughts. He had been so involved in this case that he had missed all the build up to the big day, which was only a fortnight away. He loved Christmas. Even at 19, he still found something magical about the event. He was looking forward to opening his presents — his parents could still spring a surprise with their choice of gifts. He was also looking forward to going for a lunchtime beer with his dad. Most of all, he was looking forward to Christmas lunch.

Beth was coming over. Four months had passed since he had asked her out but it felt only like last week. He still got goosebumps when they met. It had been five days since he had last seen her and he hadn't been able to phone her because of work. He was missing her company and looking forward to catching up. He had bought her the necklace she had shown him in the High Street jewellers. And some perfume and bath smellies. He couldn't wait to see her face.

As he stepped onto the pavement, a few cars swept past, their tyres swishing through the melting snow. A thaw had started. He glanced at his watch as he began the mile-long walk home.

What a week it had been. One he wouldn't forget in a long time.

A NOTE TO THE READER

Dear Reader,

The writing of *Hunter* came to me as an afterthought — the idea spawned after I had finished writing book number five in the Hunter Kerr series, set 17 years after this novel. With each book, I was developing Hunter Kerr as my central character but as I came to the end of book five I realised that except for giving brief mention as to his reason for joining the police — the brutal killing of his first girlfriend — I hadn't much of a back story of what had shaped a naïve young cop into becoming a frontline murder detective, and it was that thought, together with a folder of previously written crime fiction material to hand, which sparked the growth of *Hunter*, the novel.

In the late 1980s I had my first introduction to a writing group. I was then a uniform patrol Sergeant and so attended them whenever I could — generally during day's off or between shift patterns. Following transfer to a crime team and then drug squad I continued to dip in and out of writing groups, usually between investigations, which was a wonderful environment for relieving stress. As well as learning how to construct a novel, this gave me my first opportunity to share my early drafts of crime fiction stories, which gave me the encouragement to write more and develop my ideas.

Most of the tales came courtesy of my own experiences as a young cop, together with those of colleagues, and by the early 1990s I had a folder full of rich material, some humorous and some pretty gruesome, that I deemed worthy of progressing. And so began the process of writing my first police procedural novel. It took me eighteen months in all, most of it tucked away in a disused police cell during lunch breaks. The finished article was titled 'Loitering with Intent' and though it fell far short of being a novel, it had all the structure of a book led by a central character which was loosely autobiographical.

For years it sat on a shelf, occasionally being picked up to read pieces from it to remind me of where Hunter Kerr was first born, and it was upon taking it off the shelf after I had finished *Shadow of the Beast* — the fifth Hunter Kerr novel — that I had the thought of progressing this to be the prequel story to the series.

Many elements of Hunter are true, based on my own and former colleagues' experiences — I did battle with a burglar I caught in the act, and myself and a colleague did help push a stolen car, only saving our embarrassment by catching the culprit in a car chase, and my police radio saved me from serious harm when a villain on the run tried to stab me — though I have taken liberties with some of the drama.

I'd love to think that readers will embrace Hunter Kerr and his casework and one of the ways you can let me know that is by placing a review on **Amazon** or **Goodreads**. And, if you want to contact me, then please do so via **my website**.

Thank you for reading.

Michael Fowler

www.mjfowler.co.uk

Sapere Books is an exciting new publisher of brilliant fiction and popular history.

To find out more about our latest releases and our monthly bargain books visit our website:
saperebooks.com

Printed in Great Britain
by Amazon